Stephanie Olds

ANNETTE :
A DREAM REBORN

Annette: A Dream Reborn by Stephanie Olds

Printed in the United States of America
First Edition—Second Printing, May 2025
ISBN: 978-1968178055

Ink and Revival Publishing
Virginia, USA

Annette,

Your unbreakable strength, boundless resilience, and unwavering courage to dream have been the guiding light in my life. Through every challenge and triumph, you've shown me what it means to face life with grace and determination. Your spirit inspires me daily to pursue my own dreams with the same fearless heart you embody.

Thank you for being my rock, my role model, and my greatest source of love. I am endlessly grateful to know you.

With all my love,

TABLE OF CONTENTS

Chapter 1: Keeping Your Head Above Water 1

Chapter 2: Getting Away 11

Chapter 3: Making A Way 25

Chapter 4: Outta Nowhere 35

Chapter 5: Scratching and Surviving 45

Chapter 6: Letting Go 59

Chapter 7: The Only Way Out................................. 73

Chapter 8: Against The Storm 87

Chapter 9: The Shift In The World 99

Chapter 10: Dreams On Lockdown 111

Chapter 11: The Final Push 123

Chapter 12: New Foundations 139

CHAPTER ONE

KEEPING YOUR HEAD ABOVE WATER

The neighborhood Annette called home was a tangle of cracked sidewalks and rusting chain-link fences. Houses stood as best they could, leaning like weary old men, their exteriors peeling and bruised by time. The streets hummed with life but not always the kind you wanted to be around—idle teenagers posted up on corners, exchanging nods with passing cars, the occasional blare of sirens cutting through the thick, humid air. The smell of frying grease, exhaust, and overripe garbage mixed together in the breeze. Trash blew across the pavement like tumbleweeds, carried by the same unrelenting wind that made the wooden window frames in their house groan at night. This was home. Not because they wanted it to be, but because it was all they had.

Annette's parents worked too hard to have so little. Her mother, Sheila, pulled double shifts at the hospital as a patient care technician, where she changed sheets and comforted patients who looked at her like a ghost. Then, without a moment to breathe, she mopped marble floors in a glass-walled office downtown, where people who made six figures barely acknowledged her. Their family car—a wheezing, sputtering thing—was as tired as she was. Many mornings, it refused to start at all, leaving her to run half a mile to the nearest bus stop, hoping she wouldn't be late again. Then, some nights, she caught a ride with a co-worker, praying their old sedan wouldn't stall at a red light. Other nights, she waited for the last bus, standing under the flickering streetlamp, gripping her purse tightly.

Her father, Lawrence, was a structural engineer who worked contract jobs, designing blueprints for buildings he would never afford to step inside. In college, he had been a standout in his architecture program, praised for his innovative designs and sharp eye for detail. Professors spoke of him with admiration, convinced he was destined to start his own firm one day. He had once believed that too, spending late nights drafting visions of buildings that could reshape skylines. But life had taken him down a different path. Obligations mounted, and dreams dimmed under the weight of bills and family responsibilities. Still, he never let go of one vision—the house he had designed for his own family, the home he swore he would build with his own hands. His slim frame sagged with exhaustion some nights, but his mind never stopped sketching houses they couldn't afford to build, the edges of his notebook filled with rough outlines of homes with wraparound porches and chimneys that would never send up smoke.

Sherry and Lawrence met at an HBCU, a place where ambition and history intertwined in every brick and lecture hall. He was the quiet dreamer studying architecture, his sketchbooks filled with impossible buildings, while she was the spirited nursing student who made even the dullest anatomy lectures feel alive.

Their courtship was a whirlwind—one year of shared late-night study sessions, whispered dreams about the future, and long walks across campus, where they imagined the life they would build together. When Lawrence proposed, it felt like the next step in a carefully laid-out blueprint. But life had its own designs. A complicated pregnancy forced Sherry to leave school before finishing her degree. What was meant to be a temporary pause stretched into semi-permanence as responsibilities mounted.

Yet, through it all, they held on to their dreams— Lawrence still sketched the house he promised to build for their family, and Sherry still believed that one day, she'd find her way back to what she had started.

They owned a small piece of land sitting just outside the city limits, in a neighborhood where kids had more than cracked sidewalks to look forward to. They had set their sights on the land early, back when they were still engaged, strolling past the empty lot and imagining the home that would one day stand there. It wasn't much—just a quarter-acre of grass and promise—but to them, it represented a future they could shape with their own hands. In the mid-1990s, land in southwest Mississippi wasn't expensive by national standards, but for a young couple just starting out, the $5,000 price tag might as well have been a fortune. Still, they were determined. They saved aggressively, skipping date nights and vacations, putting away every extra dollar they could manage. By the time they had enough for a down payment, the seller was an elderly man who admired their ambition and agreed to favorable terms. Over the next ten years, they paid it off piece by piece until, finally, the land was theirs outright—a rare victory in a life full of compromises.

The streets there had trees that provided shade, and the schools had libraries with more books than dust. Annette's parents spoke of it often, as if saying it out loud could manifest the dream into reality. The land was supposed to be their future, a place where they'd finally have peace, where Annette and her siblings could attend better schools. But the years ticked by, and the land remained just that—dirt and grass, waiting for a house that would never come.

Inside their home—if you could call it that—life was a balancing act. It wasn't a house in the traditional sense; it was more of a living, breathing patchwork of necessity. Grandma Joyce's home had started small, a simple two-room structure with a tin roof and a dirt floor decades ago. But over the years, additions were tacked on like afterthoughts—rooms built when another child was born, hallways extended when there wasn't enough space, plywood walls thrown up wherever they could manage. The kitchen, oddly enough, sat right in the middle of the house, as if the rest of the home had been built around it, the smell of frying oil and simmering greens lingering in every corner.

Grandma Joyce, old but as steady as ever, kept the house running. She cooked, she cleaned, she reminded the kids that faith was free even when money wasn't.

"Hard times don't last," she'd say, stirring a pot of beans seasoned with smoked turkey necks, her gold bracelets clinking together with each movement.

"We've been making something out of nothing since the day we got here."

———

Annette had three older siblings, all wrapped up in their own worlds. Matthew, the oldest, worked part-time at the auto shop down the street and carried the weight of being the "man of the house" whenever their dad was working late. He was only 16 years old, but his hands were always stained with grease, and his shoulders always seemed a little too tense.

Jordan, the second oldest, was built like a linebacker but had no interest in sports. His head stayed buried in computers, pulling apart and rebuilding things that no one in the house understood. He spoke in half-mumbled sentences, his mind always a few steps ahead of whatever conversation was happening around him.

Then there was Chris, who didn't go by Christina anymore, the sister who wasn't quite a sister but wasn't a brother either. Chris shaved their head down to the scalp and wore baggy jeans that swallowed their frame, speaking only when necessary, their presence a quiet defiance in a world that never seemed to have the right words for them.

And then there was Annette. The baby. The quiet one. The ever-curious one who saw patterns in everything, from the way the rain hit the windowpane to the way Grandma Joyce folded laundry. She had a mind that never stopped searching, analyzing, absorbing. A gifted child, her intelligence was a seamless blend of her parents' strengths—her father's precision and problem-solving skills, her mother's intuition and compassion.

She was tall for her age, inheriting her father's height, and unlike her siblings, she preferred order. Her side of the shared room was always tidy, books stacked neatly, pencils aligned, bed made with careful hands. Meanwhile, her siblings had an aversion to cleaning, their things sprawled carelessly around the house like they belonged to the wind. Annette, however, found comfort in structure, in knowing where everything belonged. The one with her head stuck in a book while the rest of the world spun chaotically around her.

She was the only one who still listened when Grandma Joyce talked about the past. About how the government had promised things it never delivered. About how her own father had fought in a war and still couldn't buy a house in certain neighborhoods because the GI Bill "wasn't for us." About how banks redlined whole communities, boxing them into generational struggle, keeping families like theirs in places like this.

Sherry had gotten off track with her first pregnancy, but she was determined not to let it define her future. After Matthew turned two and before Jordan was conceived, she returned to college to finish her nursing degree. It wasn't easy—juggling classes, childcare, and long nights of studying while working part-time—but she refused to let her dreams slip away completely. When she finally walked across that stage and held her degree in her hands, it felt like reclaiming a piece of herself.

She had done everything she was supposed to do—
gone to college, graduated, worked hard. Lawrence,
too. Yet, for all their efforts, the world never seemed to
meet them halfway. The weight of history was heavier
than a diploma. The systems built long before they
were born had been designed to slow them down—laws
that once barred people who looked like them from
owning property, schools that were underfunded and
overlooked, banks that denied loans based on zip codes
rather than merit. Success was tougher than it looked
for people like Annette's family, even when they
followed all the rules. It pressed on them, held them
down. They had each clawed their way into higher
education, fought against odds stacked high, only to
find themselves standing still, running on the same
treadmill as their parents before them.

———————

At night, when her mother came home smelling of
antiseptic and exhaustion, Annette was already awake,
waiting. She knew exactly what time to expect her
mother, and on the nights Sherry worked late, Annette
would quietly slip out of the shared bedroom, careful
not to wake her siblings, and tiptoe toward the kitchen.
She never revealed herself—never interrupted—but she
always watched from her hiding spot near the doorway,
just wanting to make sure her mother was home safe. It
was an instinct she had inherited from her father, a

quiet kind of compassion.

Sherry would drop her purse by the door and make her way to the tiny kitchen table, where a cold turkey sandwich waited for her—one Lawrence had made earlier, carefully wrapped in foil so it wouldn't dry out. Even on the longest days, he made sure she had something fresh and easy to eat when she got in late. She would unwrap it slowly, take small bites, savoring the taste more out of gratitude than hunger.

The kitchen light cast a soft yellow glow over her tired face as she rubbed her aching feet, scrolling through her phone, looking at photos of their land. "One day," she'd sigh, staring at the overgrown lot like it was a beacon of hope, her voice full of the kind of tired that sleep couldn't fix.

From her quiet corner, Annette heard those words every night. One day. No matter how exhausted Sherry was, she never let go of that dream. She could already see the house in her mind—the front porch where she'd sit with a cup of coffee in the mornings, the wide kitchen where she'd cook Sunday dinner, the bedrooms where her children would finally have space to breathe. It was more than just a plot of land; it was proof that they were still holding on, still pushing forward, no matter how many obstacles stood in their way.

Annette didn't know if she believed in "one day." All she knew was right now. And right now, she had schoolwork to do. Right now, she had to keep her head above water.

CHAPTER TWO

GETTING AWAY

Night draped itself over the neighborhood, but sleep refused to settle in Annette's bones. The ceiling above her flickered in the dim light of the streetlamp outside, and she lay on her back, staring up at the faint shadows it cast. Her heart thrummed with anticipation, an electric current running through her veins.

Middle school. Finally.

She turned onto her side, then her stomach, then her back again. No position felt comfortable, not with tomorrow looming so close. Her new outfit—a crisp soft-pink polo and khaki skirt—hung neatly on the closet door, the pleats ironed to perfection by Grandma Joyce. The scent of starch still lingered in the air, mixing with the faint aroma of fried okra from dinner. Her white sneakers, brand new but purchased a size too big to last her the year, sat by the edge of the bed. She had only tried them on a dozen times, practicing how she'd walk into the school like she belonged there.

Beside her, Chris snored lightly, shifting beneath the tangle of sheets. Annette held her breath, careful not to wake them as she reached for the tiny flashlight she kept hidden beneath her pillow. Clicking it on, she illuminated the composition notebook resting on her chest, its black-and-white cover already soft at the edges.

She flipped through the pages, eyes tracing over the numbers and equations she had copied from one of Grandma Joyce's old workbooks. Math made sense. It was logical, precise, never changing based on who was asking the question. If you followed the rules, you got the right answer. And in Annette's world—where rules didn't always mean fairness—math felt like something she could control.

Tomorrow, she would step into a brand-new school with lockers, multiple teachers, and a library big enough to get lost in. The thought alone sent a thrill through her, but beneath that excitement lay something else— pressure. She thought of Matthew, how his second-grade report card had nearly split their family in two. A single failing grade had turned the house into a war zone, their parents' voices rising above the kitchen table while Matthew sat silent, shamefaced.

Annette had made a decision that night, one she never spoke aloud but carried in the deepest parts of herself—she would never fail. Not a class, not a test, not even a homework assignment. If she didn't have an A, it meant she had missed something, and missing something wasn't an option.

She clutched her notebook tighter, inhaling deeply to steady her nerves. Sleep could wait. Tomorrow was coming fast, and she needed to be ready.

————————

The first sound Annette registered was the hum of Grandma Joyce's voice, low and steady, weaving through the early morning air like a thread pulling the household awake. The scent of buttered grits and scrambled eggs drifted in from the kitchen, warm and familiar, mingling with the sharp morning chill that seeped through the thin walls of the house.

Annette's eyes snapped open before the alarm clock could scream. She had beaten it. She grinned to herself, pushing the thin covers back and sitting up, her stomach fluttering with anticipation.

This was it. Middle school.

She swung her feet onto the floor, the wood cool against

her skin, and immediately glanced over at her neatly laid-out outfit. The polo, the khaki skirt—still crisp, still perfect. Her sneakers, white and gleaming, sat waiting for her like a promise.

Chris groaned from the other side of the room, stuffing their head beneath a pillow. *"Too early,"* they muttered.

"Not for me." Annette whispered back, too excited to be annoyed by her sibling's reluctance.

The house was already stirring with life. In the hallway, Jordan banged on the bathroom door. *"Hurry up, Matt!"* he hollered, his voice laced with impatience.

"I just got in here!" Matthew hollered back.

Annette grabbed her clothes and slipped out of the bedroom, weaving through the narrow hallway toward the second bathroom—such as it was. It was more of an add-on, the walls thinner than the rest of the house, the sink slightly slanted to the left from years of settling. She always thought it had a certain charm, even if it wasn't exactly fancy.

Matthew and Jordan never bothered with it, though. The bathroom was on the other end of the house, tucked away past the kitchen and the laundry room. Annette wasn't sure if it was because it was a little out of the way, or just because the two of them never had the patience for anything less than perfect. Either way, it meant she had it all to herself in the mornings.

She turned the faucet, and as expected, the water sputtered and groaned before coming to life. The bathroom might've been old, but it worked. She couldn't complain. Meanwhile, Jordan still stood at the other bathroom door yelling at Matthew, no doubt wasting his time arguing over something that didn't matter.

She dressed quickly, smoothing her skirt and tucking in her shirt just right. In the mirror, her reflection stared back at her, a mixture of nerves and excitement dancing in her eyes.

This was the first day of something new. A bigger school. A real library. Metal detectors. Teachers who didn't know her yet. A fresh start.

By the time she made it to the kitchen, Grandma Joyce was at the stove, flipping the last of the eggs while her ever present gold bracelets clinked with every movement. *"Mornin', baby girl,"* she said without turning around. *"You excited?"*

"Yes, ma'am."

Grandma Joyce chuckled knowingly. *"You been up since*

before the sun, haven't you?"

Annette only grinned, sliding into her chair as her grandmother placed a plate in front of her. A single bite of grits, buttery and smooth, melted on her tongue. Across the table, Matthew was shoveling food into his mouth like he was in a race, while Jordan scrolled through his old, cracked phone, only half paying attention to his plate.

Chris entered the kitchen with a quiet *"Good morning,"* their voice low, but they didn't pause to talk —they walked straight through, heading out the door to catch their bus, dressed in a loose hoodie and baggy jeans, the male-styled clothes they wore reflecting their identity.

Sherry entered the kitchen then, her scrubs slightly wrinkled from last night's shift, her hair pulled back into a loose bun. She pressed a kiss to Annette's forehead before moving toward the coffee pot. *"First day of middle school,"* she mused. *"You nervous?"*

Annette shook her head quickly. *"Nope."*

Sherry arched an eyebrow. *"Not even a little?"*

Annette hesitated before shrugging. *"Maybe a little."*

Her mother smiled knowingly, stirring sugar into her coffee. *"You'll be fine. Just pay attention, and don't be afraid to ask questions."*

Annette nodded, but she already knew she would pay attention. She would absorb everything. She would be great. She had to be.

Outside, the distant rumble of the school bus sent a jolt of excitement through her chest. She stuffed the last bite of eggs into her mouth, grabbed her backpack, and bolted for the door, ready to step into the next chapter of her life.

————

Annette's bus stop was always on the corner of the yard belonging to her favorite neighbor, Mrs. Eleanor Washington. "Favorite" because there was no one like her. Mrs. Washington was a sprightly 89-year-old who had lived on the corner for as long as Annette could remember. But more than just the old lady who gave out homemade cookies, she was a woman of incredible stories—and even more incredible accomplishments.

Grandma Joyce often shared stories of Mrs. Washington's past, telling Annette about how the lady had worked for NASA back in the day. She didn't just work there; she helped put rockets into orbit, like the ones that made history in the 1960s. Annette was fascinated by the idea that someone so close to her had been a part of something so big, something that changed the world.

It was hard to imagine Mrs. Washington in her younger years, sitting at a desk surrounded by equations and launch plans, with everyone relying on her sharp mind to get things right. The female mathematicians and engineers who worked at NASA, like Katherine Johnson, Dorothy Vaughan, and Mary Jackson, had been pioneers in their field, helping to make space exploration possible. Annette was sure Mrs. Washington had played a role in that too, even if Grandma never gave the full details.

And then there were the books. Mrs. Washington's house was full of them, towering stacks of worn covers and yellowed pages, with titles that made Annette feel like she was walking into a library. She had every kind of book: history, science, math, literature. Anything Annette could ever dream of learning about. The woman had a mind that never seemed to stop, always eager to learn something new or share the knowledge she had. To Annette, Mrs. Washington wasn't just a neighbor—she was an inspiration, someone who had done things that felt unreachable, even impossible.

As Annette stood waiting for the bus, she would often glance at Mrs. Washington's house, thinking that maybe one day, she could be just like her—someone who made a difference, who knew the answers to questions most people didn't even think to ask.

The school bus was a relic, the kind of thing that had seen better days but still managed to putter along. It was dented in a few places, and the faded yellow paint had long since lost its shine, revealing patches of rust underneath. The seats were cracked, the cushioning deflated, and there was always a strange smell of old plastic and sweat hanging in the air. Annette had seen much better buses on TV, but around here, this was the norm. The city never seemed to care much about the buses in their low-income areas, leaving them to get worse with each passing year.

The bus driver, a woman with a fresh-faced look, sat at the wheel, her eyes gleaming with a quiet energy. She was older, but her pixie cut made her look younger, and Annette couldn't help but admire her style. The woman had alopecia around her edges, but she feathered her hair perfectly to cover it, a sleek, tousled pixie that made her look effortlessly cool. Annette loved the hairdo, but she knew she was "too young" to pull it off. Sherry wouldn't have gone for it either—her mom wasn't big on the whole "you think you're grown" look on kids.

The first stop brought on a boy named Malcolm. He was dressed in a crisp white t-shirt and jeans, his hair freshly cut into a fade that matched his clean shoes. He was quiet, offering a quick nod to Annette as he slid into a seat, the sound of his backpack thumping against the aisle. The next stop saw a girl named Keisha, her hair shaped in a fresh twist-out that bounced as she walked up the steps of the bus. She smiled and nodded as she passed by, her light pink jacket looking perfectly pressed.

The bus ride was relatively calm. There was no loud talking or rowdy behavior, just the soft murmur of the other kids who were probably still too sleepy or disgruntled about school to do much more than glance out the window. Annette, however, was wide awake, feeling the familiar flutter of excitement as she thought about what she might learn today. She was one of those rare kids who actually loved school, who couldn't wait to crack open a new book or solve a tough problem. Most of the others on the bus didn't seem to share that sentiment.

As the bus pulled into the school parking lot, Annette's eyes widened. The building was much larger than the elementary school, its high walls and long corridors intimidating in their sheer size. The air felt different too—cooler, more serious, like something important was always happening behind those walls.

Two janitors were standing at the flagpole, struggling to raise the American flag. They looked confused, one of them holding the rope while the other tried to untangle it, but they were clearly not having much luck. Annette didn't have the heart to laugh, but it was hard not to notice their frustration.

The bus came to a stop, the engine sputtering a little before it settled into stillness. Annette stood up, grabbing her backpack and stepping off the bus with a quiet determination. She walked toward the auditorium, her eyes scanning the building as she tried to take it all in. Everything here felt new, and a little overwhelming, but Annette wasn't scared. She was ready for this.

Annette moved through the school's hallways, taking it all in. So far, she liked it—maybe even more than she expected. It was big, yes, but it wasn't overwhelming in the way she thought it would be. The classrooms were bright, the walls decorated with colorful posters that made everything feel alive. The desks were neat, each one with a fresh stack of books waiting to be opened.

The day was long, though, longer than any day she'd had in elementary school. It wasn't necessarily a bad thing—it was just that with each passing period, she had to find her next class, stand in front of a new group of kids, and give yet another introduction. *"Hi, I'm Annette,"* she'd say, again and again, trying to make a good impression, but by the seventh time, her words felt like they were on autopilot.

The lunch period was the only time she'd felt a flicker of nervousness. She had imagined all sorts of scenarios—

what if she didn't know where to sit? What if she ended up eating alone? But as it turned out, lunch was just... fine. It was neither good nor bad, just uneventful. She sat with a few girls she'd seen around, not really knowing anyone yet, but everyone was polite, and the chatter wasn't too overwhelming. It was almost peaceful, in a way.

By the end of the day, Annette was exhausted, the constant movement and the repetition of the day making her feel like she'd been in a dream. It was hard to shake the feeling that she'd done the same thing over and over again. She'd introduced herself so many times, met so many new people, figured out so many hallways and classrooms. It felt like a loop, like she was walking in circles and had somehow, at some point, forgotten what time it was. But still, she made it.

When she finally arrived home, her body a little sore from all the standing and walking, Annette was still buzzing with excitement. She couldn't wait to tell everyone about her first day. The house was already full—Mom, Dad, Jordan, Matthew, Chris and even Grandma Joyce who'd typically be outside in the garden at that time. The whole family was gathered around the table, chatting and eating navel oranges when Annette burst in, eyes wide.

"You'll never believe it!" Annette said, practically bouncing in her seat as she sat down. Everyone paused,

waiting for her to speak. She was grinning so much that even her tiredness seemed to fade away for a second. *"I love the library! It's huge! Bigger than our old one by so much. It's basically brand new, and it's not just one librarian—there are THREE! Three!"*

Everyone laughed at her enthusiasm, but Annette could see that they understood. She could already feel that the library was going to be her second home. She could already see herself spending hours there, absorbing everything she could. The way she saw it, the more she learned, the more she would grow into something better—smarter, more capable, more ready for whatever came next.

Annette had always relied on the library as her escape. It was the one place where she could truly get away from the chaos of her everyday life, a life that often felt like it was filled with booby traps at every turn. In the pages of books, she could lose herself in far-off lands, where she could travel the world, taste exotic foods, and experience adventures without worrying about the struggle waiting for her at home. Reading gave her a kind of freedom that nothing else could—a break from the never-ending challenges of her real life.

Sherry nodded, smiling at Annette's enthusiasm. *"That's great, baby. I'm so proud of you."*

Annette grinned, a sense of excitement filling her chest. This was just the beginning. She had a whole new world ahead of her, and she couldn't wait to start diving into it.

CHAPTER THREE

MAKING A WAY

Seventh grade came around, and Annette could feel the shift in the air—things were changing. While she continued to thrive in school, her siblings were finding themselves in trouble.

Jordan, for one, had been suspended for bringing a device onto campus. It wasn't a cell phone, though; it was something more unexpected—a vape tool. The kind that seemed to show up in the hands of more and more kids at school. It wasn't just any device either; it was a sleek, metallic piece that looked like something out of a science fiction movie, a contraband gadget that no one would expect in the hands of a rising 15-year-old.

Lawrence and Sherry were livid. Where did he even get

it? They couldn't fathom how Jordan had managed to sneak such a thing onto school grounds, let alone use it. He was punished, grounded for weeks, and Lawrence made it clear that there would be no excuses if this happened again.

Then there was Chris. Annette hadn't seen her sister so upset in a long time. Chris had been caught up in a protest downtown, an LGBTQ+ rally, where things had gotten tense. The police were called, and 14-year-old Chris had been nearly arrested for participating in a demonstration that had gotten out of hand. Chris was defiant, standing up for what they believed in, but their parents were worried—especially Sherry, who wanted to protect her child from a world that could be unforgiving. Annette didn't fully understand the challenges Chris faced as a part of the LGBTQ+ community, but she could see that things weren't always easy for Chris, no matter how strong they acted on the outside.

As the year went on, another blow hit the family when the old car, the one that Sherry relied on to get to work, broke down for good. The oil leak that had been slowly draining away the engine's life finally caught up with them. One morning, it didn't just stop running—it caught fire.

The car was gone, and in the chaos of it all, the fire spread to the house, damaging the roof, part of a bedroom and the living room forcing them to move into a rental property. They were all shaken, but they made do.

The new place came with a new bill, a monthly rent that stretched their already tight finances. Sherry had to ride the bus for five months while Lawrence worked every angle he could to get approved for a loan. Finally, after what felt like an eternity, he got the approval. It wasn't much, but it was enough for a used car. It wasn't perfect, but it was reliable, and it was something Sherry could use to get back to work.

All of these events showed Annette just how hard her family was working to make a way. They might not have had it easy, but they never gave up. It was the kind of struggle that Annette was learning to understand more deeply, even at her young age. And though it was hard to see her parents stretched so thin, she admired their strength. They were doing everything they could to hold the family together, and Annette was determined to do her part, even if it meant extra work at school and continuing to find solace in her books.

Little did she know, in just a few short months, the family would be tested in ways they couldn't have imagined— and it would change everything.

———

Annette was in eighth grade now, and life had started to feel almost normal again. The weight of middle school was settling into a familiar routine: homework, friends, and the occasional boy who caught the eye of her classmates. Annette's friends would giggle and gossip about which boys they thought were cute, but she didn't have the same distractions. She was laser-focused on her studies. Peer pressure didn't faze her—no boy was going to take away her time with books and learning. There were goals ahead, and she wasn't about to let anything, or anyone, get in the way of them.

But as the crisp fall air settled over the neighborhood, things at home began to shift. Annette noticed the tension, even though no one really spoke about it.

It had started with her dad's trip to New York. Lawrence had attended a highly anticipated workshop for architecture professionals from October 27 to 30, a big opportunity he hoped would elevate his career. He'd talked about it for weeks leading up to the trip, excited about the potential benefits.

For Lawrence, this wasn't just any workshop—it was a chance to network with leading figures in the architecture industry, connect with influential architects, and gain insights into the latest trends and innovations. There were plans for one-on-one sessions with mentors, where he could get advice on advancing his own designs and ideas. He also hoped to learn about sustainable building techniques and how they were being incorporated into urban design, something that had become increasingly important in the field.

Lawrence was also eager to meet potential clients and collaborators, hoping this event would lead to new projects or partnerships that could help him build his portfolio. And finally, the workshop included an exclusive tour of several notable architectural landmarks in the city—an experience Lawrence believed would give him fresh inspiration and ideas for his own work.

This was his shot at breaking into a higher tier of the profession, and he wasn't going to let anything stand in his way.

Annette wasn't sure what it all meant, but she knew it had caused some stress at home. The trip was necessary for his future, but it came at a cost. They had to sacrifice a few things to make it happen—two car payments had been put off, and the electricity bill was paid only at the bare minimum. But Lawrence was hopeful.

He came back from the trip in high spirits, talking excitedly about all the great connections he'd made. He promised the family that the future was bright, that everything would get better soon.

At dinner on October 31, the family sat down to Lawrence's favorite meal—roast chicken with mashed potatoes, his special recipe. But something was off. Lawrence took a bite and then paused.

"Well, I guess I've lost my sense of taste," he joked, his

voice light, but there was a hint of concern behind his smile.

"Guess that means your mom is still mad at me for going on that trip," he continued, trying to laugh it off.

But Annette could tell that something was wrong. He never joked about his favorite meals, especially when he was so sure about how good they'd taste. Lawrence's usual enthusiasm for roast chicken and mashed potatoes was missing, replaced by a distant, almost hollow expression. His smile didn't quite reach his eyes, and Annette felt a shift in the room that she couldn't ignore.

Sherry, usually the calm center of the family, seemed a little shorter with her words, the tension between her and Lawrence palpable. She moved through dinner like she was on autopilot, her responses curt and clipped. Annette could see the tightness in her mom's jaw, the way her fingers fidgeted with her napkin, folding and unfolding it in a way that reminded Annette of when she was upset. It was obvious Sherry was still angry with Lawrence for the sacrifices they had to make for his trip to New York. The bills were late, the car was barely hanging on, and the house felt like it was inching toward its breaking point.

But it wasn't just the trip that had her on edge. Sherry still blamed herself, deep down, for running late that morning when the car caught fire. She had rushed out the door to get to work, only to see smoke rising from under the hood moments after pulling away from the house. At first, it seemed like a small issue—just some smoke, nothing more. But within seconds, it thickened, turning black and curling into the air like a warning. Panic set in. In a rush, she drove the car back toward the house, hoping to get it far enough from the street. She left the engine running, her heart racing, and rushed inside to call Lawrence, her hands trembling as she fumbled with the phone.

Within moments, the fire spread rapidly. The smoke thickened into heavy plumes, and before she knew it, the flames were dancing across the engine, licking the hood and quickly spreading to the tires. It only took a few more minutes for the fire to consume the car completely, engulfing it in flames that licked up toward the porch. The heat from the flames was intense, and the fire leaped from the car to the wooden porch, catching the siding of the house.

The fire spread faster than Sherry had anticipated. The old, wooden house, with its dry beams and worn siding, offered little resistance. Within about 8 minutes of the first smoke, the fire had spread to the front of the house, scorching the porch and climbing up to the roof. The flames cracked through the windows of the living room and began to invade the house.

When the fire department arrived, just 10 minutes after the first call, the damage was significant. The car was completely destroyed, its metal frame twisted and blackened, the seats reduced to nothing more than charred remnants. The front porch was nearly gone, and the roof was badly scorched, with parts of the ceiling inside the house showing signs of smoke damage. The living room and one of the bedrooms were fire-damaged as well, their walls blackened by the intense heat. The smell of smoke lingered for days, filling the house with the reminder of how quickly everything could change.

The accident had felt like the last straw in a string of bad luck. The family had been through so much already, and now they were left picking up the pieces of a burned car and a damaged house.

The rest of the family sat at the table, awkwardly silent, careful not to say the wrong thing. They could feel the weight of the tension in the air, the unspoken words hanging between Sherry and Lawrence like a thick fog. It wasn't the warm, bustling family dinner they were used to. Everyone was walking on eggshells, unsure of how to navigate the storm that seemed to be brewing just beneath the surface. Chris sat with one earpiece in their ear, practically ignoring the family, their gaze fixed on the plate in front of them as they tried to shut out the world; sometimes, it felt easier to retreat into their music than face the unspoken tension around them, the frustration of not fully fitting in with either their family or them self still weighing heavily on them.

It was Grandma Joyce who finally broke the silence. She

cleared her throat, her voice steady but full of warmth as she looked between Sherry and Lawrence.

"You know, forgiveness ain't just for the other person," she said softly, her eyes softening as she met Sherry's gaze.

"Sometimes it's for you, too. We all make sacrifices, and Lord knows we've all made our share. But what matters is that we keep going. That we lean on each other, even when things get hard."

Sherry's eyes flickered with emotion, and for a moment, she looked away, blinking as if trying to hold back the tears. Lawrence reached for her hand, squeezing it gently, but neither of them spoke. They didn't need to. The weight of Grandma's words hung in the room, a quiet reminder that despite the mistakes, the struggles, and the moments of anger, they were a family. And family found a way to move forward, even through the hardest times.

Then, Lawrence sat back in his chair, sighing deeply. *"I'll be able to pay off one of the car notes with my next check,"* he said. *"And for the other, well... I'll pawn my wedding ring and the record collection. We won't lose the car. I won't let that happen."*

Annette's stomach dropped. Her dad's wedding ring? His beloved record collection? She didn't like hearing him talk like that. But Lawrence seemed resolute, as though he had no other choice. He excused himself to bed, his face looking pale, his eyes tired.

The next morning, everything changed. Lawrence didn't come downstairs right away. He was usually up early, but today he stayed in bed. Annette noticed the way he'd struggled to breathe last night, his chest rising and falling in a way that didn't seem normal. She didn't say anything, but her gut told her something was off.

"I need to go to Urgent Care," he told Sherry, the words muffled by the coughs that followed. His chest hurt. He could hardly catch his breath.

———————

CHAPTER FOUR

OUTTA NOWHERE

Day 1 – November 1

Annette had barely dropped her backpack by the door when she felt it—something was wrong. The air in the house was thick, almost suffocating, like it had been sealed shut for hours. The usual hum of conversation, the sound of the TV murmuring in the background, the clatter of dishes in the sink—all of it was gone. Silence loomed, heavy and unnatural.

The TV, which was always on, sat dark and lifeless. Even the clock on the wall seemed louder, each tick echoing through the room like a countdown to something awful.

Sherry stood frozen in the middle of the living room, her phone gripped so tightly that her knuckles had gone white. Her other hand was pressed against her forehead, fingers splayed like she was trying to steady herself, to keep her thoughts from unraveling.

Annette's stomach twisted.

"What's wrong?" Her voice came out shaky, uneven.

Sherry exhaled sharply, her shoulders rising and falling like she was trying to pull herself together before speaking. When she finally turned toward Annette, her eyes were red-rimmed, her face tight with barely contained emotion.

"It's your dad," she said, voice strained. *"He's in the ICU."*

The words barely registered. ICU. Intensive Care Unit. The place where the worst cases went.

"But... he just had a cold," Annette whispered.

Sherry shook her head. *"It's not just a cold, baby. He could barely breathe this morning. He called out of work and went to Urgent Care, but they admitted him to the hospital right after. He's on oxygen now, and they said he's getting worse."*

Annette's mind raced. Just last night, he'd been joking at the dinner table about losing his sense of taste. He had plans—he was going to pay off the car. He was supposed to be fine.

She barely noticed when her siblings trickled in, each of them reacting in their own way—silent, some asking questions no one had the answers to. No one could understand how things had escalated so fast.

The next few days blurred together, a revolving door of waiting rooms, worried phone calls, and unanswered questions. The hospital allowed only two visitors at a time, which meant a constant rotation of Sherry, Grandma Joyce, and the older siblings going in and out while Annette and Chris stayed in the waiting room, staring at beige walls and sipping from cups of lukewarm vending machine coffee.

The doctors asked the same questions over and over.

"When did the symptoms start?"

"Did he have any underlying conditions?"

"Any recent travel?"

Sherry told them about New York. Told them about the workshop. Told them that Lawrence had been fine when he left, that he'd come home talking about his future, about all the connections he'd made.

She had been frustrated with him, angry even, for making the trip when money was tight, but the moment she realized he wasn't feeling well, all of that vanished. None of it mattered anymore. Loving someone had a way of making everything else feel small, of washing away resentment in the face of something bigger. She would have given anything to go back, to un-say the sharp words, to trade every ounce of frustration for just one more normal day with him, healthy and whole.

Then she mentioned the dinner, how he'd joked that he couldn't taste anything.

That made one of the doctors pause, jotting something down on his clipboard. *"That's odd,"* he muttered. *"We'll run more tests."*

When they went through his belongings, they found the crisp business card still in his wallet—a contact from the trip, a man from China whom he'd sat next to on his flight to New York. Lawrence had even mentioned him in passing, how they had talked about architecture, how the man had given him his card in case he ever wanted to work on international projects.

The doctors barely reacted.

"Lots of viruses can cause pneumonia," one said dismissively. *"We'll keep an eye on it, but this could be*

anything."

They weren't investigating it. They weren't treating this as anything more than a severe respiratory infection.

And meanwhile, Lawrence wasn't getting better.

The weekend was long and merciless, filled with nothing but stress and waiting. There was no enjoyment, no distractions—only the suffocating uncertainty of whether Lawrence was going to pull through.

Everything had been moving so fast that Sherry hadn't even thought about work, let alone gone. Technically, she *could* leave the hospital—but morally, she *couldn't*. How could she walk away, even for a few hours, when Lawrence was lying in a hospital bed, getting worse instead of better?

But the reality of it was starting to settle in. No work meant no paycheck. And no paycheck meant no way to pay for rent, food, or even gas to get back and forth from the hospital. They were about to be without income, and that terrified Sherry almost as much as Lawrence being sick.

Grandma Joyce, always the practical one, had gently reminded her that they needed to plan some meals for the week. She'd even arranged for a neighbor to bring her to the grocery store Monday morning. It was a small act of support, but it only made Sherry more aware of how quickly their resources were running out. How long could they hold things together before everything came undone?

Day 4 – November 4

Annette had been forced to go to school that morning, but she may as well have stayed home. Her body was there, moving from class to class, but her mind was stuck in the ICU with her father. Nothing made sense—her teachers' voices blurred together, and the words on the board may as well have been written in another language. By lunchtime, she realized she hadn't eaten all day, but the idea of food turned her stomach. Everything inside of her told her that things were worse than the adults were letting on. She could *feel* it.

She tried to do what she always heard grown-ups say— "*stay in a child's place*"—but by sixth hour, a different kind of worry crept in. Both her parents had been out of work for days now. Sherry hadn't been back since Thursday, and Lawrence… well, Annette didn't know when he'd work again. It didn't take a NASA mathematician to know what that meant. No paycheck. No money. And as much as she wanted to push the thought away, it stuck to her ribs like something heavy and unshakable.

By Monday evening, the doctors made a decision—Lawrence needed to be intubated.

Annette didn't fully understand what that meant at first, but the way her mother's face crumpled when the doctor told her made it clear that this was serious.

The next time Annette saw her father, he wasn't awake. He wasn't talking. He wasn't joking about food or making promises about the car. He was still, a breathing tube down his throat, machines beeping all around him.

The doctors still had no real answers. Pneumonia, they said. Severe. Maybe a secondary infection. Maybe complications from his trip.

Maybe. Maybe. Maybe.

That alone was alarming. Maybe. Lawrence couldn't even breathe, the hospital halls were getting more crowded by the hour, yet the doctors still spoke in calm, measured tones, as if this was routine. No urgency. No real concern.

Annette didn't understand much about medicine, but even at twelve years old, she knew when something wasn't right. If the doctors weren't panicking, did that mean there was nothing to panic about? Or were they just missing something—something big?

It all seemed completely illogical.

Day 5 – November 5

By Tuesday morning, Annette didn't even have to beg to stay home from school. She had barely gotten the words out—"*I'll stay here with you, don't worry*"—before Sherry just nodded and said, "*Okay.*" No argument. No half-hearted attempt to send her to class. Just *okay.*

It was like the fight had drained out of Sherry the moment Lawrence was intubated. She barely spoke now, except when necessary, her face a portrait of exhaustion. Her hair, usually neat, was pulled into a loose, lopsided ponytail, and her clothes were wrinkled from days of wear. Annette had never seen her mother look so *worn down.*

The vending machine had become their main source of food—not that either of them had much of an appetite. Since Saturday, they had survived mostly on bags of stale potato chips, peanut butter crackers, and off-brand candy bars. Every now and then, Sherry would force herself to drink a cup of hospital coffee, even though Annette could tell she barely tasted it.

Annette's piggy bank had been their saving grace. She had grabbed it on Saturday, stuffing it into her backpack without telling anyone, figuring that a few extra dollars couldn't hurt. It wasn't much—mostly quarters and a couple of crumpled bills from birthdays and chores—but right now, it felt like a fortune. Each time she slid coins into the vending machine and watched the snacks drop down, she felt a tiny flicker of control, like she was *doing something.*

But even that wasn't enough to shake the dread that sat in her stomach. The machines beeped, the nurses whispered in passing, the monitors in Lawrence's room kept up their steady rhythm—but underneath it all, silence loomed. The kind that filled every space, growing heavier by the hour.

And Annette knew, deep in her bones, that they were bracing for something worse.

Then, something shifted—but not in a way that brought relief.

The hospital halls were *even busier.* Nurses moved faster. More beds were being filled.

That afternoon, while Annette and Sherry sat in the waiting room, a doctor rushed past them, murmuring something to another physician.

"Another one? That's the third today."

Annette's ears perked up.

By the time evening fell, they overheard an update from a passing nurse—twenty more people had been admitted with the same symptoms as Lawrence. *Twenty.*

The doctors were starting to look worried now, but not because of Lawrence alone. They had a bigger problem on their hands.

One of them sighed as they passed by.

"Looks like it's going to be a rough flu season."

———

CHAPTER FIVE

SCRATCHING AND
SURVIVING

Day 9 – November 9

Annette had never known silence like this before. The hospital room was still, except for the rhythmic hiss of the ventilator pushing air into her father's lungs. The machine breathed for him now.

Grandma Joyce had been the backbone of the family that week, steady and unshakable, even as everything around them seemed to be falling apart. She wasn't the kind to break down in front of everyone, but Annette had caught her more than once just sitting at the kitchen table, staring at nothing, whispering quiet prayers under her breath.

She made sure there was *some* kind of structure, made sure everyone had something to eat—though no one was really hungry—and even managed to get a neighbor to drive Sherry to the hospital on the days she didn't have the strength to drive herself.

Chris was struggling with the weight of everything happening, particularly with their own internal battles around identity and the chaos of their family's situation. For a few years they've been distant, retreating into their own world as a way to cope, using music and isolation to shield them self from the overwhelming emotions they doesn't know how to process. The tension around Lawrence's condition had made them retreat even more.

As for visiting Lawrence, they had been to the hospital a few times, but each visit felt like a battle. It's hard for them to face their father in this state, especially with the unresolved issues surrounding their gender identity and their perception of how their family views them. The hospital is a place of overwhelming emotion—uncertainty, sadness, and guilt—and for Chris, it's harder to face that while also struggling with how they fit into the world around them. They go, but there's a distance between them and the situation.

They're dealing with all of this the best way they know how: by pulling back, keeping their distance, and focusing on anything that feels like an escape, even if it's only temporary.

Matthew and Jordan, though, were dealing with everything the only way *they* knew how—by *not dealing with it at all*. They kept their distance, not because they didn't care, but because caring *out loud* meant admitting how bad things really were. They went through the motions at home, playing video games, helping Grandma when she asked, even making small talk with Annette about school as if everything were normal. They kept their heads down, pretending if they moved through life like nothing had changed, maybe nothing really *had* changed. They had stopped asking for updates on Lawrence, stopped talking about the hospital visits altogether. If Sherry or Grandma Joyce started discussing ventilators, oxygen levels, or doctor's reports, one of them would quickly find an excuse to leave the room.

"He's gonna be straight," Jordan had said when Annette had tried to bring it up one evening. His tone was casual, almost dismissive, but Annette didn't miss the way his knee bounced under the dinner table, restless and uneasy. *"Y'all stressing for nothing."*

Matthew wasn't much better. When their uncle called to check in and asked if he'd been up to see Lawrence, Matthew had just shrugged and said, *"Nah, I'm letting the women handle that."*

It was easier to act like they didn't care, easier to pretend that staying away was some kind of strength.

"Men don't cry," Grandma had muttered that evening, shaking her head as she watched them retreat to their room after dinner. *"They think if they don't say it, it ain't real."*

But Annette knew the truth. They weren't indifferent. They were *scared*.

They were thinking the same thing she was—that something was really, *really* wrong. They just didn't want to say it out loud.

Because saying it made it real.

And it *was* real.

It was *that bad*.

Day 10 – November 10

The doctors said Lawrence was in a now coma, but they didn't have any clear answers about when—or *if*—he would wake up.

Sherry sat beside his bed, fingers laced together so tightly that her knuckles were screaming. She barely spoke, barely moved, barely ate. The vending machine money had run out yesterday, and Annette wasn't sure if either of them would have touched real food even if they had it.

Annette watched her father's chest rise and fall with the help of the machine, trying to remember the last time she'd seen him animated, laughing, *alive*. Just over a week ago, he had been joking about dinner. About paying off the car. About a brighter future. Now, he was trapped in this state, tethered to machines, and no one seemed to have answers.

A nurse came in to check his vitals, but Annette already knew what she would say. No change.

It was getting harder to believe that there ever *would* be a change.

Day 11 – November 11

The tow truck came before sunrise.

Annette had woken up on the couch to the sound of tires crunching over gravel. At first, in the haze of half-sleep, she thought she was dreaming. But when she heard the metallic *clank* of chains, followed by the deep rumble of an engine, she bolted upright.

By the time she made it to the window, it was too late.

The car was already hooked up, its front tires lifted off the ground, headlights casting long shadows across the damp pavement. Sherry came stumbling out of the house, barefoot, wearing an old t-shirt and pajama pants. Her voice cracked as she called out—*"Wait! Please, I can make a payment! Just give me another day!"*—but the repo man didn't even look at her.

Annette pressed her forehead against the window, stomach knotting as she watched her mother plead.

The man shook his head, barely sympathetic. *"It's already processed, ma'am. It ain't personal."*

It *was* personal.

The car—the one Lawrence had been fighting so hard to keep—was gone.

Annette had always known things were bad, but seeing her mother, desperate and helpless in the early morning darkness, made it all too real. Dad was in the hospital, maybe dying. Mom had been missing work for days. Now they didn't even have a way to *get* to the hospital without asking for rides.

Annette backed away from the window, stomach churning, and sank down onto the couch.

They were *really* losing everything.

———————

Lawrence had really gambled when he used money to go to New York. It hadn't even been a full two weeks before the bottom had fallen out. The car was history, repossessed without so much as a second glance. Past-due bills were showing up in the mailbox every day, each one a heavy reminder of the family's dwindling resources. It had seemed like a good idea at the time—Lawrence had *believed* in the future, in those business connections and workshops that were supposed to set everything in motion. But now, as he lay in a coma, that hope felt like a distant dream. All the sacrifices they'd made for that trip—missing car payments, letting the bills slide—had been in vain.

By Day 14, things were getting worse. Matthew had used the funds from his paycheck to buy meat and pay the water and gas bill. He was working part time, but the family was in debt, full time. Annette and her siblings were grateful just to get breakfast and lunch at school. It was the only real meal they could count on, the only break from the growing hunger that sat in the pit of their stomachs every day. The meals were simple—nothing fancy—but they were filling, and right now, that was enough.

Grandma Joyce had been doing her best to stretch what little food they had left, but even she was starting to worry. The cupboard was nearly bare, and the fridge wasn't much better. She'd been cooking up "struggle meals"—the kind of dishes that you made when you were trying to make do with what was left.

Pork and beans and rice, but no hot dogs. Just the beans and rice, with a little salt to give it flavor.

Eggs and rice, the most filling option, but not quite as comforting as they used to be.

Rice and butter, with just a touch of sugar to make it taste like something sweeter than it really was.

Oatmeal.

And, sometimes, just butter and sugar with a little bit of cinnamon, on stale, toasted bread.

It wasn't much, but it was all they had. And Grandma made it work, as best as she could. Still, there was a worry in her eyes that Annette noticed more each day. She could see it when Grandma handed out the portions at dinner, her hands shaking ever so slightly as she dished up what little remained.

"Lord help us," Grandma would say softly as she set the table, though her words were more prayer than complaint.

Annette didn't say anything, but she could feel the weight of it. The silence was growing heavier, not just in the hospital room, but in the house, in their stomachs. They were surviving, but just barely.

Day 18 – November 18

Annette woke up with an ache in her stomach so deep it almost felt personal. Mondays were always the worst. The school breakfast would have to repair the starvation damage from the weekend, or she wouldn't be able to concentrate at all. Hunger made everything harder— thinking, moving, even existing.

She had gotten used to it, in a way. The gnawing emptiness in her stomach was just another part of life now, like dodging past-due notices on the counter or pretending not to see the worry in Sherry's eyes. But even if she was used to it, she hated it.

By the time she got to school, all she could think about was food. She barely noticed what was going on around her until the scent of warm cinnamon rolls and eggs hit her nose. Relief washed over her as she grabbed her tray, finding a quiet seat to eat. The first few bites felt like survival.

But even after breakfast, the weight of everything at home sat on her shoulders like a loaded backpack she couldn't take off.

By fourth period, Annette had managed to shake off some of the morning's exhaustion, but she still wasn't fully there. The math teacher, Ms. Castillo, stood at the front of the classroom, holding a flyer in her hands.

"Alright, listen up," she said, her tone carrying the forced enthusiasm of a teacher who already knew what kind of reaction she was going to get. *"There's an opportunity coming up—one that could change someone's life."*

That got a few half-hearted glances from the class, but most students barely looked up.

Ms. Castillo pressed on. *"This June, there's a nationwide mathematics competition open to middle and high school students across the country. It'll be held downtown from June 15th through the 19th, and the first-place winner gets a $50,000 cash prize."*

Silence.

Not the kind of silence that meant people were thinking, or processing, or even pretending to be interested. It was the heavy, dismissive kind, the kind that told Annette the room had already checked out. A few kids snickered under their breath. Someone in the back muttered, *"Ain't nobody doin' no extra math."*

"Ain't nobody got time for that", another student added.

Ms. Castillo sighed. She had expected this, but it still disappointed her. She knew the environment she was working in—knew that for most of these kids, the idea of a math competition wasn't even in the realm of possibility. Survival came first.

She looked over the class one last time. *"If anyone is interested, come see me after class,"* she said, trying not to sound defeated.

No one moved.

Annette sat there, barely registering what had just been said. She was too distracted, too consumed by the endless thoughts of her dad in the hospital, her mother's exhaustion, the emptiness in their kitchen.

But something about *$50,000* stuck in her mind.

After school, Annette didn't go to her bus.

She wasn't ready to step back into that house, to sit in more silence, to pretend that everything wasn't crumbling. So instead, she found herself outside, standing in the parking lot, watching as Ms. Castillo walked toward her car.

"Ms. Castillo?"

The teacher turned, surprised. *"Annette?"*

Annette hesitated for only a second before squaring her shoulders. *"That competition... how do you enter?"*

Ms. Castillo blinked, her face shifting from confusion to something softer—pleasant surprise. *"You're interested?"*

Annette nodded.

Ms. Castillo studied her for a moment, like she was trying to understand why Annette, out of all her students, would be the one to care. Then, she smiled. *"I'll get you the details tomorrow. But Annette, this isn't just a test you show up for. You'll need to study—prepare."*

"I will," Annette said quickly. *"I'll do whatever it takes."*

And she meant it.

As she walked home that evening, the sun dipping below the horizon, she felt something she hadn't felt in a long time.

Hope.

She would enter this competition.

And she would win.

Because if she didn't, her family would fall apart.

CHAPTER SIX

LETTING GO

Day 26 – November 26

Things hadn't improved—not even a little.

It was clear now, even if the doctors hadn't said it outright. They weren't trying to *save* Lawrence anymore. They were just *managing* him, keeping his body going until it couldn't anymore. Every time a doctor came in, their updates were short, their voices calm but empty. No new treatments. No new plans. Just the same tired words—*"We'll keep monitoring him."* But for what? Annette could see it in their eyes. They were just waiting.

The family was starting to realize it too, though no one had the heart to say it out loud. They moved through their days like ghosts, barely speaking, barely eating, barely *being*. It was like they were frozen in place, caught between the life they had before and the one they knew was coming, but didn't want to face.

Annette was learning something in real-time—something that no one had ever told her about grief. It wasn't just sadness. It was *confusion*. It was watching someone who had been alive, *real*, just days ago, turn into a person who no longer existed in the present, only in memories. It was looking around at a family who didn't know how to be a family anymore without the person who held them together.

Some family members had quietly put the unspoken pieces together. One afternoon, Aunt Delores showed up at the hospital with a cardboard box of fried chicken and dinner rolls, her only explanation being, *"Y'all gotta eat."* A couple of days later, Cousin Ronnie stopped by the house and dropped off a steaming pot of spaghetti with no mention of why he'd come.

It was the kind of thing people did when they knew a funeral was coming before it had even been planned.

But food didn't make things any easier. The air in the house was still thick, heavy with everything no one wanted to say.

And back at the hospital, there was nothing left to do but wait.

Annette had fallen asleep in the hospital chair again. The kind nurse had brought her a blanket earlier, but it didn't stop the stiffness in her neck or the cold in the room from seeping into her bones. She stirred at the sound of soft voices—whispers that felt heavier than usual.

Her eyes blinked open. Sherry was sitting by the bed, holding Lawrence's limp hand in both of hers.

Something was wrong.

Annette sat up, her heartbeat suddenly loud in her ears. Her father's chest, which had been rising and falling with the help of the ventilator for weeks, was *still*. The machine let out a long, low beep.

The world seemed to slow down as a nurse stepped forward, pressing her fingers gently to Lawrence's wrist, then looking up with a quiet nod.

Sherry let out a soft, broken sound—half gasp, half sob— before burying her face into their intertwined hands.

He was gone.

Annette's breath hitched. She wanted to say something, to reach for him, to do *anything*, but her body wouldn't move. The weight of it crashed down on her like a heavy wave, drowning out everything else in the room.

Day 27 – The Lights Go Out

The house was dark.

Not dim, not quiet—*dark*. The kind of darkness that swallowed everything whole, the kind that made their home feel smaller, emptier, *wrong*.

The power had been shut off that afternoon. Sherry had called to pay it, but the woman on the phone had sighed and told her, *"I'm sorry, ma'am, but you missed the service cut-off time. The next appointment isn't until after the holiday on Monday, five days from now."*

Five days.

So now, they sat in the dark, waiting.

The last bit of money they had was already gone. No paycheck was coming. No extra hours for Sherry to pick up, no savings to fall back on. Just overdue bills everywhere, unopened envelopes filled with threats of disconnection, and a checking account so empty it may as well have been a void.

Sherry had tried her best not to let it show, but Annette could see it—how overwhelmed she was, how every breath she took seemed to carry the weight of it all. Some nights, after the kids had gone to bed, she would sit at the kitchen table with her Bible open, staring at the words but not really reading them, hands clasped together like she was trying to physically hold onto her faith.

"God will provide", she had whispered once when Grandma Joyce asked how they were going to make it. But even as she said it, her voice wavered.

Faith didn't pay the bills.

Faith didn't put food on the table.

Faith didn't bring the power back on.

Still, it was all she had left.

The fridge sat uselessly in the darkness, filled with nothing but half-empty condiment bottles and a jug of water. The food pantry donations were running low, and Sherry and Grandma Joyce had stretched what little they had as far as it could go. But stretching didn't create food where there was none. The struggle meals were turning into just *struggle*.

And yet, nobody complained.

Chris sat on the couch, scrolling through their phone, earbuds in, pretending not to be listening—but Annette knew better. Chris was always listening, always absorbing. They just didn't know how to react, how to *be* in a house that felt like it was closing in on itself. They had been avoiding long conversations, avoiding eye contact, avoiding *feeling* too much. It was easier to retreat, to keep their emotions locked behind the walls they had built over the years.

When the lights went out, Chris had just sighed, pulled their hoodie tighter around their face, and muttered, *"Man, this some bullshit."*

Not loud. Not angry. Just matter-of-fact.

Because it *was* bullshit.

Jordan and Matthew weren't saying much, either.

Jordan spent more time outside, headphones in, pacing the porch like he was waiting for something—though Annette wasn't sure what. Maybe for someone to fix this. Maybe for Dad to come home, walk through the door like nothing had happened. Maybe just for *time* to pass, so he could get past this part of his life.

Matthew had been quiet, too, disappearing into the room for hours at a time.

Then, he shocked them all when he came out with an envelope, silent and unreadable as he placed it on the kitchen table. It wasn't until Sherry opened it that the truth came out—he had been secretly saving money for a car, little by little, scraping together **$3,000** from odd jobs and side hustles.

It was his own hard-earned ticket out of there, but when the funeral home called needing upfront payment, he handed it over without hesitation.

"It's just money," he had said, voice gruff. *"We need it more than I do."*

Annette saw the way Sherry looked at him then—pride mixed with sorrow, gratitude tangled with grief. She had nodded, her lips pressed tight, unable to say the words forming in her eyes.

And now, that money had bought them the dignity of laying Lawrence to rest properly, but it hadn't bought light, or warmth, or relief from the growing emptiness in their home.

That night, they ate peanut butter sandwiches by candlelight, barely speaking.

There was no Thanksgiving that year.

The Funeral – December 2

They got dressed in the dark.

Sherry had managed to buy them all something appropriate to wear—black dresses for her and Annette, suits for the boys, and Chris. Even Lawrence had a sharp black suit to be buried in. But the power was still off, so they fumbled through the morning with flashlight beams and cell phone screens, moving in silence as they buttoned and zipped and tied.

The funeral home smelled of flowers, strong enough to make Annette's stomach turn. It was small, nothing extravagant, but nice enough. The casket stood at the front of the room, glossy and polished, but Annette couldn't bring herself to look at it just yet.

She sat stiffly in the pew beside her brothers, her hands clenched together in her lap. The service passed in a blur—words of comfort, prayers, snippets of Lawrence's life that felt like echoes of something she wasn't ready to let go of yet.

Sherry held herself together, but Annette saw how her hands trembled when she wiped at her eyes. Grandma Joyce sat beside her, murmuring soft *Amens* and squeezing her daughter's shoulder.

When it was time to leave, Annette overheard something she hadn't expected.

"The insurance covered everything," Sherry said to Grandma as they stood by the door, *"but that was it. It's all gone."*

All *$10,000*. Every last bit of it.

Annette had always known funerals were expensive, but hearing that the money was *gone*—completely, entirely gone—made something inside her tighten.

There was no cushion left. No safety net. Just a house full of bills, an empty chair at the dinner table, and a grief so thick that none of them could breathe through it.

———

The next few weeks seemed to merge into one another.

The food pantry became their lifeline. Sherry had gone back to work, but only part-time—she wasn't ready, and everyone knew it. The bills piled up faster than the paychecks could keep up.

So every Saturday, Grandma Joyce took the bus with Annette to the food pantry, standing in line with dozens of other families, waiting for brown paper bags filled with canned goods and day-old bread.

Getting there wasn't easy. It took *three* different bus transfers, each one dragging them farther from home and deeper into the parts of town where struggling families gathered, hoping for just enough food to make it through the week.

The trip was long—nearly two hours one way—and the waits at the transfer points felt even longer. Annette would sit on the cold metal benches, shifting uncomfortably, trying not to let her stomach growl too loudly. And more often than not, she'd spot a familiar face in the crowd.

A classmate from math. A boy who sat two rows behind her in science. A girl she'd once worked with on a project, now standing in line with her mom, looking anywhere but in Annette's direction.

Nobody ever said anything.

Nobody ever made eye contact.

They all understood the silent rule—*we don't talk about this at school.*

Annette wasn't embarrassed—not really. Hunger had a way of humbling you.

At home, the air was always thick with tension. No one knew what to say, how to move forward. Sherry spent most nights sitting at the kitchen table, staring at Lawrence's old paperwork, flipping through unpaid hospital bills with dead eyes.

Matthew stayed out late, avoiding the house as much as possible.

Before Lawrence got sick, he had always seemed to enjoy being the "acting man of the house" whenever their father worked late or was away. He took pride in fixing things around the house, giving Jordan, Chris, and Annette advice they didn't ask for, and handling small tasks that made him feel grown. He liked the *idea* of responsibility—the kind he could step into when it suited him and step out of when it didn't.

But now? Now that the role had been *permanently* handed to him, Matthew wanted no part of it.

At just 17, he was staring down the weight of something he wasn't ready for—leading an entire household through the worst moment of their lives. His mother was drowning in grief, his siblings were looking to him without realizing it, and the world had given him no time to process what had happened. Lawrence had always been *there*, and now he wasn't. And that absence—permanent, unfixable—was terrifying.

Psychologists called it *role engulfment*, when a person's entire identity gets swallowed by an expectation placed on them. Maybe that's what was happening to Matthew. The thought of being "the man of the house" had once felt like a badge of honor—something he could wear proudly while still having the safety net of his father beneath him. But now, that net was gone, and the badge was suddenly a burden, a label that meant *everything* fell on his shoulders.

So he disassociated. He stayed out late, spent more time with friends, played basketball until the court lights flickered off, anything to keep from going home and *feeling* what was happening. If he didn't talk about it, if he didn't sit in that heavy silence with the rest of them, maybe it wouldn't be real.

Maybe if he kept moving, kept running from it, he wouldn't have to admit the truth—

He was *not* ready for this.

Jordan sat on the couch with his headphones in, staring at the TV but not really watching it.

Chris barely spoke at all.

And Annette—Annette buried herself in anything that *wasn't* the suffocating weight of grief. She read, she scribbled math problems in the margins of old notebooks, she tried to disappear into something, *anything*, that wasn't this.

The silence stretched on, and the sadness settled in.

They were surviving.

But just barely.

CHAPTER SEVEN

THE ONLY WAY OUT

The new year came and went without excitement. No fireworks, no resolutions, no feeling of a fresh start—just more of the same. The same stress. The same unpaid bills. The same cold house, where everyone moved like shadows, too drained to talk about how bad things really were.

And now, school was back in session.

Annette took her usual seat on the bus, watching as kids piled in, laughing and showing off their Christmas gifts. New sneakers. Designer hoodies. The latest smartphones. Shiny jewelry that glinted under the dull winter sun. Some of the younger kids even had brand-new backpacks, as if Christmas had come with a fresh start.

It was strange—but not surprising.

Their neighborhood was low-income, but every year after Christmas, it was the same thing. Parents who barely had enough to keep the lights on would find a way to buy their kids *everything*—flashy, overpriced, and often completely *useless* things. Maybe they used up their savings. Maybe they maxed out credit cards. Maybe they even wrote bad checks, knowing the consequences would catch up to them later.

It was all about appearances.

Annette understood it, but at the same time, she *didn't*.

She had never been the kind of kid who cared about flashy clothes or name-brand shoes. What good was a pair of Jordans when your mama couldn't afford rent? What was the point of a new phone if your fridge was empty? Unlike her classmates, Annette *knew* the value of a dollar.

She watched them, laughing and showing off, but she didn't feel envy. Just a quiet sort of detachment, like she was observing another world—one she didn't belong to.

By the time the bus pulled up to school, Annette was already thinking about something else.

The morning dragged on, one class blending into the next. Annette didn't speak much, didn't engage in small talk like some of the other students.

Instead, she focused on what mattered.

Before her fourth-hour class with Ms. Castillo, she made a quick stop at the library. It had become her refuge, a place where she could block out the noise and focus. She walked past the shelves, scanning for any books that might help her prep for the competition, anything to sharpen her mind. She ended up grabbing an old pre-calculus workbook, even though she wasn't technically at that level yet. She figured if she could master the hardest problems, the competition wouldn't stand a chance.

She sat at a table in the farthest corner, flipping through pages, letting numbers replace the worries in her mind.

By the time the bell rang, signaling the start of fourth hour, Annette took a deep breath, tucked the book under her arm, and headed to Ms. Castillo's class.

She was *ready*.

Annette walked into her math class expecting *something*—a reminder about the competition, maybe, or at least a final push from Ms. Castillo to get someone—anyone—to sign up. But the teacher didn't mention it. The flyer was no longer taped to the board, and no one brought it up.

The math competition had become just another forgotten opportunity, buried beneath the reality of a school full of students who had bigger problems than solving equations.

But Annette hadn't forgotten.

That *$50,000* prize was burned into her mind. It was a number that could change everything. A number that could save them.

That night, she sat on the edge of her bed, balancing Sherry's old laptop on her knees as she registered herself before the 'January 15' deadline. The laptop ran slow, its fan whirring loudly in the quiet room, but it still worked.

She was using the Wi-Fi from the Patton's house across the street—sometimes it cut in and out, forcing her to reload pages and wait impatiently. But tonight, the signal was strong. *Stronger than usual.*

Annette took that as a sign.

She filled out every field carefully—name, school, grade level, home address. Her hands shook slightly when she clicked **Submit**.

A second later, the confirmation email arrived.

She exhaled. She was in.

A week later, a thick envelope arrived in the mail. Annette tore it open, her heart pounding. Inside, she found a *participant package:*

- A welcome letter congratulating her on entering
- Details about the competition structure
- Practice materials—stacks of equations and word problems, meant to test every skill she had

She set up at the kitchen table immediately.

Every day after school, she studied. Every weekend, she practiced. Numbers, equations, theorems—each problem felt like a puzzle waiting to be unlocked, and Annette was determined to crack them all.

But not everyone was happy about it.

"Annette, did you wash the dishes like I asked?" Sherry's voice was sharp, exhausted.

Annette barely looked up from her notebook. *"I'll do it later."*

"You'll do it later," Jordan mocked from the couch. *"Man, all she do is scribble in that notebook."*

Matthew, who was scrolling on his phone, muttered, *"Let her be. Ain't like she in the way."*

Annette swallowed hard but didn't argue.

Because, *yes*—she thought exactly that.

Them numbers *were* going to pay the bills.

She had been reviewing and practicing every single day, and for the first time in a long time, she felt confident about something. Confident in a way that hunger, grief, and darkness couldn't shake. She could see the problems clearer, solve them faster. The numbers made sense. More sense than anything else in her life.

But she knew Sherry wouldn't understand.

Not now.

Not after Lawrence had chased a dream that ended up killing him.

Sherry wouldn't see this as a way out. She would see it as another risk—another dangerous leap of faith when they couldn't afford to gamble on *anything*.

Annette wasn't sure how to tell her family about the competition, and because she knew how callous Jordan could be, she decided not to say anything at all.

Not yet.

For now, she would just study.

And when the time came, she would let winning do the talking.

Before Sherry could press the issue, Grandma Joyce spoke up from the kitchen. *"Let that girl study."*

Sherry sighed, rubbing her temples. *"Mama, we all got responsibilities. She can't just—"*

"I said, let her study." Grandma's voice was firm. *"You and me both know that girl ain't out in these streets, she ain't running 'round wasting time. She's trying to do something."*

Sherry didn't answer.

Annette wanted to tell them—*I'm doing this for us.* But instead, she picked up her pencil and kept working, letting numbers drown out the noise.

_____

It was late when Annette heard the argument.

Chris and Sherry had been going back and forth for nearly an hour, their voices cutting through the house like knives.

Annette didn't catch the whole fight, but she heard pieces:

"You don't even see me, Ma!"

"Chris, I don't have the energy for this right now—"

"You never have the energy for it! For me!"

Then the slam of the front door.

Annette exhaled and flipped to the next practice problem.

Chris was gone.

Not just *out* for a walk or cooling off. *Gone.*

Hours passed. Then a full night.

By morning, panic had set in. Sherry was calling everyone she could think of. Grandma Joyce sat at the kitchen table, flipping through her Bible, rubbing her temples. Matthew and Jordan kept checking their phones, pretending they weren't scared.

Annette didn't move from the table.

Chris was her sibling, and she loved them. But Chris *wasn't* her problem.

Annette had calculated the situation and made her decision—Chris would either come back, or they wouldn't. Either way, it wouldn't put food in the fridge or keep the lights on.

She *had* to stay in a child's place.

So she kept studying.

By the time Chris came back **24 hours later**, the house had sunk into exhausted silence.

The door opened, and there they stood—looking tired, looking defeated, looking *relieved* to be back.

Sherry was the first to move. *"Where the hell have you been?!"*

Chris didn't answer.

They dropped their bag by the door and took a deep breath. Then, finally, they muttered, *"I didn't wanna be here."*

It was the most honest thing they'd said in weeks.

Sherry's anger deflated instantly. She sighed, rubbing her hands over her face.

Grandma Joyce stood from the table and walked over, wrapping Chris in her arms. She didn't lecture them. Didn't demand answers. Just held them tight, rubbing circles into their back, whispering, *"It's okay, baby. You're home now."*

Chris buried their face in Grandma's shoulder, gripping her shirt like they might fall apart.

And maybe they already had.

The first sob came quietly, like they were testing to see if it was safe to let it out. But once it started, there was no stopping it. Chris wasn't just crying about running away. They were crying out *years* of pain—of feeling unseen, of carrying the weight of who they were in a house that had never fully understood them.

It was tough enough just existing in their shoes. Tough enough navigating the world as a Black transgender teen, feeling like they had to fight for space in their own home. But to feel like their own mother didn't even have *time* for them? Like Sherry's grief over Lawrence had swallowed whatever energy she might have had left for her children? That hurt in a way Chris couldn't even put into words.

So they didn't try.

They just *cried*.

Annette had never seen them like this before. Chris was usually so guarded, keeping their emotions tucked away behind sarcasm, music, and the occasional outburst. But tonight, none of that was there.

Tonight, Chris was *relieved* to cry.

Annette could see it in the way their body shook, in the way their fingers clung to Grandma Joyce's back like they were afraid she might let go. She could hear it in the way their breath hitched between sobs, the way their voice cracked when they tried to say something but gave up and just *let themselves feel*.

And Grandma Joyce? She just held them. She didn't rush them, didn't shush them, didn't tell them to pull themselves together.

She just kept rubbing their back, whispering the same, *"It's okay, baby. You're home."*

Annette watched the moment unfold from the kitchen table, gripping her pencil a little tighter.

She understood why Chris had left.

She also understood why she *couldn't*.

───────────

Later that night, after Chris had showered and gone to bed, Annette sat at the table, flipping through her practice book. The house was quiet now.

The last couple of days had been a blur of tension and silence. Sherry had become more and more withdrawn, hardly speaking to anyone, her gaze distant and tired as she sat in front of bills that no one could pay. The weight of Lawrence's death was still crushing her, but Annette knew there was more to it—Sherry was struggling with the reality of not knowing how to hold the family together. She was stretched too thin, trying to keep everything from unraveling. The anger Annette had seen in her mother's eyes those first days after Lawrence passed had turned to exhaustion, frustration, and a quiet *despair*.

Then, Chris had run away. Annette had felt a knot in her stomach as Sherry called every friend, every family member, anyone who might know where Chris had gone. But by the time Chris came back, it was almost as if nothing had happened—except that everything had.

Annette knew that Chris was grieving too. It was written all over them. But what hurt even more was how Chris had been left behind—ignored by the people who should've been taking care of them. It was tough to be in their shoes, and Annette knew that the loneliness Chris had been carrying was finally spilling out.

And Ms. Castillo hadn't even mentioned the competition again.

The competition Annette had been preparing for, the only real thing she could *hold on to*, the one thing that might actually give her family a fighting chance. Ms. Castillo's class had become a place where Annette had to force herself to pay attention, even though all she could think about was the next practice problem in her workbook, the next step in her preparation. Annette had expected her teacher to mention the competition—maybe even check in with her to see if she was still planning to enter. But the silence from Ms. Castillo felt like just another reminder that no one cared, that no one was paying attention to her goals.

It felt like everyone older than Annette was losing their grip. Her mom was too consumed by grief to manage anything, Chris was running away from their emotions, and the adults around her were barely holding it together.

Annette swallowed the frustration bubbling in her chest.

Everyone's falling apart, she thought, but there was no time for that.

She was the only one who seemed to be holding on. So she kept flipping through her practice book, one page after another, working through every problem with a determination that felt different now. A new kind of fire burned in her belly—because if she didn't do this, *who would*?

She had to make this happen. She had to prove that she was different, that her family could survive this, and she would be the one to get them through.

No one else was going to do it.

Not her mother. Not Matthew. Not Jordan. Not Chris.

Annette sat at the table, the weight of the world pressing down on her shoulders, but she didn't stop working. Because she wasn't just studying for a math competition. She was studying for her family's future.

And that was everything.

She solved one problem. Then another.

Every number, every equation—it all made sense. Unlike life, unlike grief, *math had rules*. Math had answers.

And Annette was going to use it to save her family.

Because she had to.

CHAPTER EIGHT

AGAINST THE STORM

February was brutal.

The snow came down in sheets, coating the streets in a layer of icy white that made everything feel cold—not just the outside world, but everything inside the house as well. The old grey snow, heavy with grime from the streets, was like a blanket that smothered the entire town, making everything feel dull and lifeless. Snow was rare in Mississippi, but they were over it. The once-bright winter wonderland had turned into a dreary, slushy mess, and it weighed down on people's spirits.

Even the trees, half-buried under the heavy load of snow, looked defeated, their branches sagging with exhaustion. The sky was the same cold grey, not a hint of blue, and it never seemed to lighten, casting a heavy, oppressive shadow over everything. The whole world felt *glum*, like it was trapped in a perpetual twilight, never quite waking up.

It wasn't just the weather. It was the way everyone in the family seemed to be moving through the motions, stuck in their own heads, their own sadness, with no escape from the dreary rhythm of it all. No one had the energy to clean, to cook, to talk. The snow weighed them down just as much as the bills, the grief, the silence.

Annette couldn't help but feel it—the cold leached into her bones, not just from the outside, but from everything that was happening at home. It was hard to stay focused, hard to stay hopeful when everything felt frozen. Even the days she had off from school felt like they had no meaning—just one long stretch of nothing, everything covered in layers of dirty snow.

School was canceled more days than it was open. The air had the same damp, cold feel to it inside as outside, and the sense of time slipping away was palpable. Annette lost track of the snow days by the time the sixth one rolled around, each day stretching into the next like they had no end. The once comforting sound of snow crunching beneath shoes had turned into a reminder of how stagnant things had become—how everything was on pause.

The teachers seemed just as disoriented as the students, their expectations low, their patience worn thin. The cracks in the system were visible everywhere—teachers didn't have the time, resources, or energy to really teach, and students weren't able to focus long enough to absorb anything. This generation of children had been conditioned to pay attention in short bursts, their attention spans whittled down by endless distractions—social media, video games, and a world where everything could be consumed in seconds. Anything longer than a minute or two, and they'd stop focusing, drift off, or zone out completely.

The students were never really *engaged*, just barely keeping their heads above water, doing just enough to get by. It was a constant struggle to stay on track, especially when nothing felt like it mattered. No one in class seemed to care about the lessons, and the teachers, defeated by the endless cycle, had stopped trying to motivate them. The lessons were empty, lifeless—teachers half-heartedly passing out worksheets, their voices monotone, trying to hold the attention of a room full of kids who had already checked out.

The empty remarks about *"nobody getting anywhere"* if they didn't put in the effort were often spoken in a weary tone, as though the teachers were more trying to convince themselves of something they no longer believed. Every day felt like a repeat of the last—lessons that no one took in, homework that barely got turned in, and test scores that reflected the apathy that had grown like weeds in the system.

Annette could feel it too. It wasn't just her classmates. She was *tired*, too. Tired of hearing the same dismal expectations, tired of trying to focus on a world that seemed to be moving too fast for anyone to keep up with. She had heard teachers talk about how this generation of kids was different—how their focus depth and cognitive aptitude had shrunk, how their interest in learning had faded, how school had become more about survival than actually *learning* anything.

And yet, Annette still kept at it. She kept studying, kept pushing through. It wasn't because she had to. In fact, for years, Annette had sailed through most of her classes without hardly even trying. She pulled straight A's without breaking a sweat, barely having to open a textbook to ace a test. In her early years of school, she had genuinely believed she was a *genius*, maybe even Mensa-level—at least, that's what she told herself. Every answer seemed easy. Every problem was a puzzle that practically solved itself in her mind.

But as the years went on, Annette began to realize something unsettling. It wasn't that she was some kind of academic prodigy. It was that *no one else* seemed to care enough to even try. Her classmates, her peers—they were barely doing the bare minimum. Their work was sloppy, rushed, or incomplete, and even when they *did* turn something in, it was half-hearted. Annette had always been a standout, but it wasn't because she was smarter than everyone else. It was because she was the only one who actually *cared.*

She had been a part of a generation that didn't seem to care about much of anything—*not their health, not their futures, not their education, nothing.* Their lives were lived in a haze of apathy, drifting from one thing to the next with no real intention or focus. Some of them couldn't even get out of bed in the morning to make it to school, and those who did only came because their parents told them to.

The more Annette observed, the more she understood. Her classmates didn't struggle because they weren't smart— they struggled because they didn't want to be there. They didn't want to learn, didn't want to engage with what was right in front of them. The system was full of kids who had no drive, no passion, no spark for something more. They were stuck, their futures slipping away because no one had taught them the value of effort. No one had shown them that learning could be the key to something bigger.

Annette realized that her effort, her willingness to do the work, wasn't an anomaly. It was the exception. And it made her feel more isolated than ever. She was doing her best, working as hard as she could, but she felt like she was trying to swim upstream in a river of indifference. The people around her weren't fighting. They weren't even trying to stay afloat. They were just... existing.

And so, Annette kept pushing through. She kept studying, kept working on her goals. But for most of her peers, it was like watching a slow-motion train wreck.

She sat in the back of the classroom most days, her notebook open, but her mind was elsewhere. There were too many problems at home. Too many things that didn't make sense. She was trying to stay focused on the math competition, but it felt like everything around her was falling apart, and she had no idea how to stop it.

Sherry had found a way to cope—by just barreling through. She was working more than ever now—three jobs. She wasn't sleeping, barely eating, and still finding time to come home at night, only to leave again after a couple of hours to take on the next shift. As a reminder to them all, her schedule was posted on the refrigerator:

5 a.m. to 1 p.m. – Greenhill Grocery & Deli

2 p.m. to 7 p.m. – Bright Horizons Caregiving

8 p.m. to 12 a.m. – SunnySide Cleaning Services

Annette tried to keep track of it, but it was impossible. Sometimes, she felt like Sherry was just passing through the house, moving like a shadow between shifts. It was hard to imagine how much longer this could go on. The work was wearing her thin, and it was clear that there were holes forming in her ability to hold it together. She had no time to stop and think about anything other than surviving.

They had food, utilities, and medicine. But even that felt tenuous. The rent had been missed for two months now, and the landlord had made it clear that *partial payments* weren't acceptable. The eviction notice came just days after Valentines Day, adding another weight to their already-burdened shoulders.

Annette had overheard the conversation between Sherry and Grandma Joyce about it.

Sherry's voice had been tight with exhaustion, barely holding it together as she talked about maybe having to find a different place to live.

"I don't know, Mama," she said, her tone rough with frustration. *"Maybe it's better if we just move. Find a place cheaper, get away from the rent that's already behind... maybe we could start fresh."*

But Grandma Joyce wasn't so sure. *"It ain't that simple, Sherry. You think moving's gonna be easier? We'd need new deposits, application fees, reconnection fees for the utilities. Hell, you'd be starting all over again, and we ain't got that kind of time or money right now."*

Sherry was quiet for a long moment, the weight of it all pressing on her. *"I know... I just don't know what else to do. I'm not gonna keep taking this from him. He won't even let me pay towards what I owe."*

She wiped a hand over her face in frustration. *"And the way things are going, we might not even make it through this month."*

Grandma Joyce exhaled slowly, her voice steady despite the exhaustion she was carrying too. *"The only thing we can do is find a way to **pay what we owe**. You stay focused on that—everything else is just distractions right now. You can't afford to be starting over somewhere new."*

Sherry let out a defeated sigh. *"I just wanted us to have some peace. To have something steady."*

Annette listened, her chest tightening as the conversation unfolded. She knew it wasn't just about the money—it was about the strain it was putting on Sherry, the weight of trying to juggle it all without any real help. In the end, moving wasn't ideal. It would cost more than they had. Their only option was to scrape together enough to pay the rent they already owed, even if that meant sacrificing everything else.

Annette wanted to say something—wanted to promise that things would get better—but all she could do was stare at her math book, biting her lip, feeling the weight of everything she couldn't fix.

One evening, as Annette sat next to Grandma Joyce on the couch, the news blared in the background. The reporter spoke in calm, measured tones about a growing health crisis overseas:

> *"...an outbreak in China, affecting thousands, many reporting difficulty breathing... hospitals overwhelmed with patients... The Centers for Disease Control have confirmed that the U.S. is not at risk... there's no need to worry."*

But Annette couldn't help but wonder. What if this was it? What if this was the reason Lawrence had gotten sick so quickly? The man he'd met on his flight to New York—hadn't he mentioned something about working with clients from China? Annette had never heard Lawrence talk so enthusiastically about a connection before, a person he'd met on a flight, but now it all seemed so... important. So strange.

Was that how this all started? Was that the reason her father had gotten sick, and why they couldn't figure out what was wrong with him?

Grandma Joyce's voice interrupted her thoughts. *"It's far away, baby,"* she said, patting Annette's hand. *"Don't need to worry about it. We've got enough to deal with right here."*

Annette nodded, but the doubt lingered. *Could this be the reason?*

Despite everything happening at home, Annette stayed *laser focused* on one thing—her math competition.

No one knew she was studying for it.

Sherry was too consumed by her endless shifts to notice. The long hours, the exhaustion, the absence at home—it was all consuming. Even when Annette sat at the kitchen table late into the night, Sherry barely glanced in her direction. The light from the kitchen lamp cast long shadows, but Sherry's tired eyes didn't take notice.

Chris, still distant after everything, wasn't interested in asking what Annette was up to. Their silence spoke volumes, but it didn't reach Annette, who was too deep in her studies to notice or care. Chris seemed to be somewhere else, in their own world, their own grief, unable to be present.

Matthew, as usual, was lost in his own world. He would come home late at night, barely acknowledging the rest of the family. Annette could hear him pacing in the room, his music blaring, his thoughts always elsewhere. He had *checked out*—a quiet retreat into avoidance.

And Grandma Joyce? She didn't ask about the competition, not in any real way. She'd never been the type to dig for details, but she'd seen the way Annette focused, the way the math books stayed open on the table. She saw the commitment, the quiet persistence. While she didn't know the specifics, she knew that something was driving Annette—something more than schoolwork. And so, she just quietly encouraged her studies, without asking *why* they mattered so much, but giving Annette the space to pursue it in her own way.

As for Jordan, he was just... Jordan. He didn't say much these days, even less than usual. He would come and go, headphones in, per usual, barely acknowledging the tension in the house. Annette had stopped trying to talk to him about anything meaningful, knowing it wouldn't get through. He seemed to be doing his best to block out the world, just like the rest of them.

No one else had the energy or the will to ask questions or offer support. But she didn't need it.

Annette spent hours every evening, after the rest of the family had gone to bed, poring over the practice materials that had come with her registration. She sat at the kitchen table, working in the dim light of the one lamp that still worked. Numbers, equations, formulas—they made sense to her. The pages in the workbook felt like a lifeline.

She had to do this.

She couldn't explain it, but she knew that the math competition was more than just a chance to win money. It was her way out. If she won, things could be different. She could change everything for her family.

And every time she solved another problem, it felt like one small victory against the chaos of their lives.

CHAPTER NINE

THE SHIFT IN THE WORLD

March – The World Turns to Panic

The first signs of panic crept into the U.S. like a slow-moving storm. At first, it was just murmurs—news stories from overseas, whispers about a virus that was spreading. But then, one day in March, everything flipped. Schools closed. Businesses shut down. Streets emptied. The world was on lockdown, and no one knew what to expect next. The shelves in grocery stores were bare. The air felt heavier, colder, like the entire country was bracing itself for something catastrophic.

Annette's family watched the news with a mix of disbelief and fear. The virus was here. It was real. But it wasn't the same virus they had heard about just a few weeks ago, the one that the news had barely taken seriously. Back then, they'd brushed it off—*No need to worry, the U.S. is prepared. It's just a flu-like illness, and it's far away.*

Those words felt like a cruel joke now, as the virus spread faster than anyone had predicted. What had seemed like an overseas issue was suddenly knocking on their door.

Now, the broadcast showed footage of hospitals overwhelmed with patients, makeshift wards set up in convention centers, doctors and nurses wearing makeshift gear, trying to protect themselves from a virus that was *not* just a bad cold. It attacked the lungs. It made it impossible to breathe. Annette saw images of people gasping for air, lying in hospital beds, their bodies frail and struggling, as the death toll climbed each day. The numbers were rising, and it didn't matter how much the government tried to downplay it—*this* was real. This virus, this pandemic, had become a reality that everyone had to face.

Grandma Joyce had muttered earlier that week, *"The world's never seen anything like this,"* and now, Annette could feel the weight of it. They hadn't taken it seriously enough back then. They should have been worried.

Here they were, all stuck in the middle of it, in a world that was changing faster than they could understand. Sherry—who had barely been able to stay afloat before— found herself losing her three jobs all at once. The deli. The cleaning service. The caregiving position. Every job she had begun to rely on was gone.

"How are we gonna make it now, Ma?" Annette heard Jordan ask quietly one evening, his voice tinged with fear.

Sherry didn't have an answer. She had been exhausted before the pandemic, her body worn thin from working three jobs to make ends meet. Now, without any work, there was nothing but silence in the house.

The bills kept coming, but now there was no paycheck to cover them. Sherry had been on the phone for hours, dialing one number after another, trying to figure out how to apply for unemployment benefits and food assistance. The process was a maze of long hold times, confusing websites, and unanswered questions. She'd never had to do this before—Lawrence had always been the one to handle things like paperwork and financial assistance. He knew the ropes, could talk to anyone with ease, and had a way of making difficult processes seem simple. Sherry missed him so much it hurt, and now, faced with the challenge of navigating the bureaucracy alone, she felt completely overwhelmed.

She would hang up the phone after each call, her shoulders slumped with frustration. The knowledge that Lawrence would have known exactly what to do, how to talk to these people, how to fill out the forms without second-guessing himself—it was like a sharp ache in her chest. He had always been her partner, her guide through the hard times. Now, without him, everything felt like an uphill battle.

Annette could see it too. Her mother's face had become a mask of exhaustion—her eyes were bloodshot and the spark of hope that had once burned bright in them was completely gone. Every day, Sherry's energy seemed to drain a little more, the weight of it all—of the bills, the unknowns, the loneliness—pushing her down. The house felt quieter now, more somber, as if it too was bearing the weight of uncertainty. Annette could feel it pressing in on her, a heaviness that hung in the air, making every breath a little harder, making each day feel longer than the last.

But there was one small piece of good news: evictions were halted. The landlord couldn't kick them out for the time being, but it didn't change the fact that they were living on the edge. The future was uncertain, but for now, they were safe.

As the days stretched on, the world outside became more and more surreal. Annette's school clumsily switched to remote learning—if you could even call it learning. Teachers were scrambling to adapt, sending out emails and assignments without knowing how to deal with the overwhelming chaos. Some of the lessons felt like a half-hearted attempt to maintain some semblance of normalcy, but the connection was unstable, both literally and figuratively.

At home, Annette had her mom's old laptop, the one that still worked—but the Wi-Fi from the house across the street was far from reliable. Sometimes it would work fine, allowing her to download assignments and check emails. But other times, the signal would drop out mid-lesson, leaving her staring at the screen, waiting for the little spinning circle to stop and bring her back online.

Frustrated, Annette emailed her teachers about the Wi-Fi situation, explaining that she was doing her best to keep up with the work but couldn't always access the materials. It wasn't long before Ms. Castillo replied with a bit of hope. She had already heard about families struggling with internet access and promised she would try to find a way to get Annette access to free Wi-Fi at home or through a community program. It wasn't a perfect solution, but it was something. Annette couldn't help but feel a little bit of relief, knowing that Ms. Castillo cared enough to help—even if there wasn't much that could be done right away.

As the days passed, the uncertainty loomed. Annette, meanwhile, still had a single focus—*the competition.*

The math competition she had been preparing for was still on, as far as she knew, but the entire world felt like it was in freefall. How could she study when the libraries were closed, and she had no books? She had left some of her study guides in her locker at school when everything shut down. At first, she thought she'd be able to get back to them in a week or two. But now, with everything up in the air, she didn't know what to expect. She couldn't access all of the materials she needed, and the uncertainty was eating away at her.

She had memorized most of the concepts, the formulas, and the steps, but how could she prepare without the practice problems? She didn't even know what the competition would look like anymore. How would they hold it in the middle of a pandemic? She was so **lost**—doubting herself, wondering if her dream was just too ambitious in the first place. Maybe it was stupid to even try.

It all felt like a distant fantasy. In the face of the pandemic, with so many things out of her control, Annette wasn't sure what she was doing anymore. Her mom was struggling, and the world felt like it was falling apart. Who could focus on something like a math competition when the reality of a pandemic, unemployment, and the future of her family was on her shoulders?

April – A Glimmer of Hope

The world outside was quieter now, the streets eerily empty. The smell of disinfectant lingered in every store and every hallway. No one knew how long this would last. Days turned into weeks, and Annette's anxiety continued to mount. She couldn't focus on schoolwork, couldn't focus on anything except the feeling that the dream to win the competition was slipping further away.

One day, she decided she needed to get out of the house. She grabbed a disposable mask and her jacket and headed down the street to Mrs. Washington's house, her favorite neighbor, a woman who had always been sweet, kind, and encouraging, full of stories and wisdom. Mrs. Washington had a house full of books —books that Annette had admired every time she visited. Maybe, just maybe, she could find something—anything—that would help her with the competition.

But when she knocked on the door, it was answered by a relative of Mrs. Washington's, a granddaughter who hadn't been there when Annette had stopped by before.

She stood in the doorway, a woman in her mid-30s or low 40s—Annette couldn't quite tell because her pecan-brown skin was so taut and flawless, with a subtle sheen to it that glistened in the dim light. Her hair was a mix of smooth, controlled curls with several rogue strands of grey springing out from the edges, as if they had a mind of their own. The rest of her hair was laid perfectly in place, neat and contained, though the grey hairs told a different story of time passed.

She wore an oversized sweat suit, clearly chosen for comfort, the fabric a soft, faded shade of charcoal. Her French-manicured nails gleamed even in the low light, immaculate and precise. The scent of fresh soap and a hint of lavender clung to her, a calming presence that felt almost like a hug before she even spoke.

"Hi, honey," she greeted Annette with a warm, open smile. Her voice was gentle, smooth, welcoming. Just like Mrs. Washington had been.

But even with her kind demeanor, Annette knew something wasn't right. She noticed the way the woman's smile didn't quite reach her eyes, the slight tension in her posture, the way her fingers fidgeted nervously with the door frame as if she were searching for the right words.

Annette's gut twisted. There was a quiet sadness in the air. Something was wrong—something she couldn't quite place yet, but it made the pit of her stomach tighten with unease.

"Mrs. Washington is in the ICU," the lady told her quietly, shaking their head with sorrow in their eyes.

Annette's heart dropped. *"What happened?"*

"They're not sure yet. She's been sick for a while. We're all worried. But she's getting care."

The lady sighed. *"I'm sorry, baby. But you can't come in right now."*

Annette felt a pang in her chest. Mrs. Washington had always been there, always full of advice, always a source of light in their neighborhood. Now, she was in the hospital. It was hard to process. She knew what the ICU meant. She nodded silently, feeling a strange mix of relief and sadness. She couldn't help but feel like the world was taking everyone she cared about, one by one.

She left the house quietly, her heart heavy. It wasn't that she didn't want to help or be there for Mrs. Washington. It was just that, in this time of uncertainty, she didn't know where to put herself.

———

Two weeks passed. Annette still hadn't heard anything about the competition, and school was becoming a distant memory. The anxiety about the future continued to build inside her. But she hadn't forgotten about Mrs. Washington. Every day she thought about going back to her house, hoping to see the familiar face, hoping to find some comfort.

One afternoon, she did go back. But when she reached the house, she saw that things were different. People were moving boxes out, packing up her neighbor's belongings. Annette stood still for a moment, her heart pounding. She stepped onto the porch, unsure of what to say.

"Is Mrs. Washington okay?" she asked softly, her voice barely above a whisper.

A relative looked up from the boxes, their face strained with grief. *"She... passed away three days ago. We're just clearing out her things now."*

The words felt like a punch. Mrs. Washington, the woman who had been a quiet beacon of stability, was gone.

Annette didn't know what to say. But she had to ask. *"Can I have her books?"* she asked, her voice cracking slightly. *"I—I could really use some right now."*

The relative seemed surprised by the request but nodded slowly. *"She would've wanted you to have them. Take whatever you need."*

Annette didn't waste any time. She started loading up the rusty wagon she found in the yard, packing it full of books that Mrs. Washington had kept over the years. She could tell some of them were old, some were worn out, but all of them felt like treasures—like pieces of knowledge that she could still use to fight through this storm.

When she returned home, she went straight to the backyard, the old wagon squeaking beneath the weight of the books. She hadn't even thought about anything else in the world except getting these books. As she sifted through them, her heart skipped when she found a few math textbooks tucked between the mixture of novels and old magazines.

There were algebra books, geometry books, and even a few advanced problem-solving guides. These weren't just random books. These were *gems*—perfect for her to use as she tried to figure out how to succeed in the competition.

Her hands shook as she began flipping through the pages, discovering that Mrs. Washington had kept books that spanned years of learning, from basic to advanced. She had everything she needed now—right in front of her.

Annette smiled. The dream wasn't over. It was still very much alive.

CHAPTER TEN

DREAMS ON LOCKDOWN

April – A Strange New Normal

The world outside remained chaotic. The streets were quieter than Annette had ever known them to be—no kids playing, no basketballs bouncing on the pavement, no music blaring from car windows. Just silence, except for the occasional ambulance siren in the distance.

Inside the house, though, things had *finally* settled into something that resembled stability.

For the first time since Lawrence died, Sherry wasn't drowning under the weight of stress. With the unemployment checks coming in regularly and food stamps loading onto the card each month ensuring they had enough to eat, the house wasn't filled with the same gut-wrenching anxiety it had been before. They weren't thriving, but they weren't on the verge of eviction either.

Sherry still hadn't found another job, but in a way, that was a blessing. The world was shut down—businesses closed, schools barely functioning, the news reporting an endless stream of fear and uncertainty. *No one* was really working unless they were deemed "essential," and even those jobs were dangerous.

The world outside was still a mess, but their little house finally had a moment of peace.

Annette was using every second of it.

And Sherry could breathe.

She had time.

She had the luxury of sitting on the couch in the early afternoon, watching the news with Grandma Joyce, drinking coffee instead of rushing out the door to one of her three jobs. She even laughed sometimes now. Not often, but more than before.

It was in one of those rare moments of calm that she *finally* acknowledged Annette's intense focus.

Each morning, after eating breakfast and helping Grandma Joyce clean up, Annette would sit at the kitchen table with her stack of books—the ones she had hauled home from Mrs. Washington's house. The pages were old, yellowed at the edges, and some of the books still smelled faintly of the lavender Mrs. Washington used to keep in her drawers. Annette didn't mind. She spent hours poring over equations, solving problem after problem, scribbling in a worn notebook that was quickly filling up with numbers and notes.

Sherry had walked past the dining table dozens of times without saying anything, but that day, she stopped. Annette was hunched over a notebook, scribbling furiously, muttering numbers under her breath, her brows furrowed in concentration. There were textbooks spread out in front of her, filled with tiny, precise notes in the margins.

Sherry crossed her arms. *"Alright, Annette, I gotta know— what are you doing? Every time I look up, you're buried in them books."*

Annette barely looked up. *"Studying."*

Sherry smirked. *"That much? You got a secret boyfriend sending you coded messages in that notebook?"*

Annette groaned. *"Ew, Mom. No."*

Grandma Joyce chuckled from her recliner. *"Leave that child alone. You know Annette don't care about boys."*

Sherry shook her head, but her eyes softened with curiosity. *"Alright, then tell me. What's got you more focused than a preacher on Easter Sunday?"*

Annette barely looked up, finishing her equation before responding. *"I'm studying for a math competition."*

Sherry blinked. *"A math competition?"*

Grandma Joyce perked up from across the room. *"Oh? What kind of competition?"*

Annette sat up straighter. She *beamed.* She had been waiting for this moment—waiting for someone to ask. She grinned, flipping to a clean sheet of paper.

"Okay, so—" She pulled out the official flier from the participant packet and placed it in front of them.

"There's this nationwide mathematics competition. It's open to middle and high school students, and it's going to be held in person, downtown, in June, and I already signed up for it back in January."

She started drawing a huge **$50,000** in bold letters at the top of the page.

And the first-place prize is *fifty thousand dollars.*

Sherry raised an eyebrow. *"Fifty thousand?"*

Annette nodded enthusiastically. *"Yes! And I already registered. I've been practicing for months. I got these books from Mrs. Washington's house—may she rest in peace—and I've been working through them every day."*

Both Sherry's eyebrows lifted. *"You signed up? By yourself?"*

"Yeah," Annette nodded, eyes bright. *"And I've been studying for months."*

Sherry sat down hard in the chair across from her. *"Fifty*

what?"

"Thousand," Annette repeated, her voice steady, confident. *"If I win, we can pay off everything—catch up on rent, pay all the bills, stock up on food. We won't have to struggle anymore."*

Sherry stared at her for a long moment before shaking her head with a small laugh. *"Baby, I love you, but you got a better chance of goin' to the damn moon."*

Grandma Joyce reached over and smacked her arm. *"Sherry!"*

"What? I'm just saying!" Sherry held up her hands, but Annette wasn't fazed.

Sherry exchanged a glance with Grandma Joyce, her expression unreadable. *"And what makes you think you can win?"*

*"Because I'm **smart**, Mom,"* Annette said, as if it were obvious. *"I know I can do it. And if I win, I can help us."*

Sherry sighed and ran a hand down her face. She knew Annette was intelligent, but *this?* It sounded like a dream too big for reality—like something people from *other* neighborhoods won.

But before she could say anything, Grandma Joyce spoke up, nodding firmly. *"She **can** do it, Sherry. And if she believes in it this much, you oughta believe in her too."*

Sherry exhaled, looking back at her daughter. Annette's

eyes were bright, filled with something that had been missing for a long time—*hope*.

"*Alright*," Sherry said, forcing a small smile. "*Go win the thing, then.*"

"*I know I'm going to win,*" Annette said simply. "*I've been practicing every single day. I know the material better than I ever did in school. I just need to keep working, and when the time comes, I'll be ready.*"

Grandma Joyce smiled warmly. "*Well, I believe in you, baby.*"

Annette turned to Sherry, waiting.

Sherry sighed and gave a small, tired smile. "*I mean, I guess if anybody could do it, it's you.*"

Annette took that as a victory.

May – School Becomes a Joke

By May, school had completely unraveled.

Teachers had given up. The school had tried to hand out laptops, but there weren't enough to go around.

The district had abandoned their efforts on trying to enforce attendance, and most students had stopped logging in altogether. Annette still checked the school portal occasionally, but the assignments were nonsense.

Worksheets with no real instruction. Videos from teachers who didn't know how to explain lessons over Zoom.

It wasn't worth her time.

So she stopped signing in.

She dedicated her full days to studying math.

Every morning, while other kids were still asleep or aimlessly scrolling through their phones, she was working through algebra problems, testing herself on geometry, pushing herself further than she ever had before.

The libraries were still closed, but she didn't need them. She had everything she needed in the books from Mrs. Washington's house.

June – A Visitor on the Porch

By early June, Annette had all but given up on hearing about the competition again. With the world still upside down, she assumed it had been canceled.

At first, she tried not to let it bother her. After all, she had spent months sharpening her skills, stretching her mind in ways she never had before. The knowledge she gained wasn't useless. Numbers weren't tied to one opportunity. Math would always exist, and the things she had learned would stay with her. Maybe one day, she could put them to use in another way—maybe at another competition, maybe at college, maybe even in a career.

But that logic only went so far.

The real reason she had been studying so relentlessly wasn't just for the sake of learning. It was because her family needed that prize money *now*. They weren't worried about the future—they were worried about today, about next month's rent, about whether they'd have to rely on food stamps forever. Annette hadn't been studying for a theoretical success in some distant future. She had been fighting for survival, and now that chance was slipping away.

A sense of disappointment settled over her, but she refused to let it turn into defeat.

Annette had always had a practical mind, the kind that could assess a situation and adapt. She understood that life didn't always bend to people's will, no matter how hard they worked or how badly they wanted something. She wasn't naive enough to think that effort alone guaranteed success. Some things were just beyond her control, and she had the emotional intelligence to recognize that.

Still, it didn't mean she wasn't frustrated.

She found herself staring at her books longer than usual, flipping through pages she had already memorized. She would run through equations in her head, not to prepare for anything in particular, but because she needed to believe that all this work hadn't been in vain.

She wasn't discouraged—not exactly. But she was tired.

And more than anything, she hated that after all the hope she had built up, after all the determination, after all the late nights spent working toward a goal, she might have to let it go.

For now.

Because no matter how brilliant she was, no matter how ready she had made herself—this wasn't something she could fix.

And that was the hardest part.

Then, one afternoon, there was a knock at the door.

Grandma Joyce pulled the door open, revealing Ms. Castillo, standing on the porch, a mask covering her face, her eyes warm and smiling. She was holding a stack of books and folders in her arms, gripping them carefully, as if they were something valuable. Even with half her face hidden behind the mask, Grandma Joyce could tell she was there with purpose.

"Can I help you?" Grandma Joyce asked, eyeing the woman with a mix of curiosity and caution.

Ms. Castillo shifted the books slightly and pulled down her mask just enough to reveal a reassuring smile before quickly putting it back in place. *"Good afternoon, ma'am. My name is Ms. Castillo—I'm Annette's math teacher at school."* She glanced down at the materials in her hands.

"I came to check on her and bring her some resources for a math competition. I wasn't sure if she had been able to prepare, so I wanted to make sure she had what she needed."

Grandma Joyce chuckled, shaking her head as she leaned against the doorframe. *"Oh, baby, you're a little late for that,"* she said with a knowing grin. She nodded toward the porch, where Annette's old, well-worn math books were stacked neatly on the table. *"My grandbaby is going to win the whole thing. She's been studying for **months**!"*

Ms. Castillo blinked in surprise, looking from Grandma Joyce to the books and then back again. *"Wait... she's been practicing?"*

Grandma Joyce gave her a look, like *of course she has.* *"Like it's her full-time job."*

Ms. Castillo let out a soft laugh, shaking her head in admiration. *"That girl... I should've known."*

Grandma Joyce turned into the house, calling out in her deep, authoritative voice, *"**Annette! Get out here, baby! You got company!**"*

A few seconds later, Annette appeared at the door, her brows furrowing when she saw Ms. Castillo standing there. She looked between her grandmother and her teacher, sensing something was up.

"What's going on?" Annette asked, stepping onto the porch.

Ms. Castillo met her eyes, still holding the books in her arms. *"Annette... we need to talk."*

Annette hurried outside, and they sat on the porch, a few feet apart.

"I had to come in person," Ms. Castillo said, pulling a paper from her bag. *"The competition is still happening."*

Annette nearly dropped her pencil. *"Wait, what?!"*

Ms. Castillo nodded. *"The sponsors decided to move forward, following Covid-19 protocols. The event will be smaller, but it's still on."* She hesitated. *"And I found out you're already registered."*

Annette grinned. *"I've been studying nonstop."*

Ms. Castillo looked down at the stack of books on the porch table and exhaled, shaking her head in disbelief. *"Annette, I had no idea... You've been working alone this whole time?"*

Annette nodded.

Ms. Castillo let out a soft laugh, her voice filled with admiration. *"You're incredible."*

From inside the house, Sherry watched through the window. She still wasn't sure this was a *realistic* dream, but as she saw the way Ms. Castillo looked at her daughter—with **genuine** pride—she realized something.

Maybe Annette could do this after all.

———————

That night, Annette lay in bed with her siblings, the moonlight creeping through the curtains.

"I know I'm gonna win," she said with absolute certainty.

Jordan snorted. *"Yeah? And what we gonna do with all that money?"*

Annette smirked. *"First, we're paying the rent back. All of it. Then, we're paying the future rent so we never have to stress about it again. Then, the bills—gone."*

Chris, scrolling on their phone, smirked. *"And toilet paper."*

"Oh yeah," Annette laughed. *"Enough toilet paper to last a lifetime."*

Jordan grinned. *"Bet. So, can I get a laptop?"*

Chris turned their screen toward Annette, showing a photo of a twist hairstyle with an insane price tag. *"I need this. It's $125."*

Annette chuckled, shaking her head. *"Y'all so basic."*

But then she grinned.

"I promise. When I win—we all win."

And for the first time in a long time, it felt like something real.

CHAPTER ELEVEN

THE FINAL PUSH

Ms. Castillo wasn't the type to leave things to chance. She knew Annette had the potential to go far in the competition, but raw talent wasn't enough—she needed training, strategy, and discipline. So, she led with a no-nonsense approach. For the next few days, Ms. Castillo became a fixture in Annette's daily routine. She would show up on the porch with a stack of worksheets, a stopwatch, and a determined expression behind her mask. She wasn't just a teacher now; she was Annette's coach, mentor, and cheerleader wrapped into one.

"You're good, Annette," she told her one afternoon as they sat at the kitchen table, a stopwatch between them. *"But good doesn't always win. We need you to be unstoppable."*

Annette nodded, pencil in hand, determination burning in her chest. Ms. Castillo would fire off questions, pushing Annette through timed problem sets, correcting her mistakes immediately.

"All right, let's see how you handle this set," Ms. Castillo said one morning, setting a timer on the kitchen table. *"You've got thirty minutes. Go."*

Annette took a deep breath and started working, her pencil scratching furiously against the paper. The problems weren't easy—Ms. Castillo made sure of that. She had combed through past competitions, gathering the most challenging questions she could find. The goal wasn't just to sharpen Annette's skills but to prepare her for the mental endurance the competition would demand.

Grandma Joyce watched from the doorway, arms crossed, nodding approvingly. *"That baby is something else,"* she murmured to herself.

It was intense, but Annette didn't flinch—she embraced the challenge. Each night, she lay in bed running equations in her head, visualizing different problem-solving techniques.

By the end of the session, Annette's fingers were stiff, her brain exhausted, but her spirit was soaring. Ms. Castillo checked the answers, nodding with satisfaction. *"You only missed two. And even those were just minor errors. You're ready."*

The morning of the competition, Annette's stomach

twisted with nerves. She sat at the kitchen table, stirring a bowl of oatmeal absentmindedly, barely tasting the cinnamon and sugar she had added. Her appetite was gone, but Grandma Joyce had insisted she eat *something*. Across the room, Matthew scrolled on his phone, nodding to some music only he could hear, while Jordan flipped through a magazine, aimlessly. Chris sat on the couch, half-watching the morning news, their expression unreadable.

Sherry was already out the door, having to leave early for a doctor's appointment. She had kissed Annette on the forehead on her way out, mumbling a quick, *"Do your best, baby,"* before rushing to catch the bus.

Grandma Joyce, sensing Annette's nerves, walked over and placed both hands on her granddaughter's shoulders. *"Baby, you done worked too hard to doubt yourself now. You walk in there and show 'em what you're made of. Ain't no reason to be nervous when you know you belong there."* She pulled Annette into a tight hug, her warmth wrapping around her like a shield.

Just then, two sharp beeps sounded from outside— Ms. Castillo's car.

Annette took a deep breath, grabbed her bag, and shot out of the house.

"Time to shine, superstar," Ms. Castillo called as Annette climbed into the front seat.

Annette nodded, death-gripping her backpack strap. *"I feel like I could throw up."*

"That's how you know you're ready," Ms. Castillo teased. *"Nerves mean you care. Now let's go win this thing. You ready?"* Ms. Castillo asked, as she pulled out of the driveway.

"As I'll ever be," Annette replied, her voice steady but her hands now fidgeting with the strap of her backpack.

The streets were quieter than usual, the weight of the pandemic still looming. Annette sat in the passenger seat, nerves buzzing under her skin.

When they arrived, Ms. Castillo gave Annette a reassuring nod before she walked in alone. Only participants were allowed inside—no coaches, no teachers, no friends. The venue was eerily silent, a stark contrast to how such an event might have felt before the pandemic. No cheering families, no excited classmates, just masked competitors standing six feet apart, waiting for their numbers to be called.

Inside Competition Hall B, the atmosphere was electric, despite the reduced number of competitors. The event was held in a large arena, its high ceilings echoing with the occasional murmur of the proctors and staff. The competition floor sat in the middle of the vast space, a sea of desks arranged in precise rows, each spaced six feet apart. Bright overhead lights illuminated the entire setup, making the polished floors gleam beneath them. The proctors, dressed in formal attire with navy-blue blazers, paced the rows, their expressions neutral yet alert, watching the competitors closely.

A total of 109 students had arrived to compete, representing a variety of backgrounds. Annette spotted students of East Asian, South Asian, African, Hispanic, Middle Eastern, and European descent, some of them speaking in hushed tones in their native languages before the competition began. Some of the competitors looked like high school seniors—tall, confident, and sharp-eyed—while others, like Annette, were on the younger side. There were noticeably more high school participants than middle schoolers, but that didn't faze her. She hadn't come here to worry about age differences. She came here for one thing, and that was to win.

Still, she couldn't help but feel slightly intimidated by a few of them—especially the ones who *looked* like money. Their designer sneakers, high-end backpacks, and expensive watches suggested they had access to the best tutors, the best prep materials, maybe even private coaching. One boy near the front adjusted the cuffs of his crisp white dress shirt, his movements so smooth it was as if he had done this a hundred times before. A girl nearby set down a leather-bound notebook and took a slow sip from an insulated bottle that definitely wasn't from Walmart. Annette felt her hoodie suddenly *too plain*, her sneakers *too worn*, but she shook it off. *Numbers don't care about money,* she reminded herself. *It's just me and the math.*

The proctors stepped to the front, their voices echoing slightly in the massive arena. *"Good morning, competitors. Welcome to the national mathematics competition. Please take your assigned seats and prepare for the first round."*

Annette took a deep breath, squared her shoulders, and walked toward her desk. She had worked too hard to let intimidation creep in now. It was time to prove that she belonged here.

Each morning, Ms. Castillo dropped Annette off at the doors. *"I'll be right here at four to pick you up,"* she reassured her each day. And every evening, Annette returned to the car, exhausted but triumphant.

Monday: Annette advanced to the next round. She solved problems methodically, tuning out the world, allowing numbers to be her guide. Ms. Castillo picked her up that afternoon, nodding in approval but keeping her praise measured. *"First round is just the start,"* she reminded her. *"Don't get comfortable."*

Tuesday: Another round, another victory. Annette's confidence grew, but so did the difficulty of the problems. She saw students around her struggle, some unable to finish their problems in time. She pushed through, her pencil never stopping.

Wednesday: By now, exhaustion was settling into her bones. The pressure was mounting. Some students cracked under the weight of the competition, but Annette remained firm. Numbers were her refuge. She *advanced again.*

Thursday: The final day of timed testing. One more test before the winner would be announced. The competition had started with dozens of students, but now, only four remained—including Annette. She collapsed into the seat, barely able to keep her eyes open. *"Final round tomorrow."*

Ms. Castillo beamed. *"You are incredible, Annette. Just one more day."*

Friday morning felt heavier, like the weight of everything leading up to this moment pressed down on Annette's shoulders. She could barely focus on her clothes as she pulled them on, the world outside feeling like a blur.

Tension thick in the air, each step to the car seemed like an uphill climb, and the tightness in her chest wouldn't loosen. It wasn't just any Friday—it was the day of the math competition, and everything depended on it.

Grandma Joyce insisted on coming along this time. *"Can't let my grand-baby go to battle without knowing I'm out here waiting,"* she had said, as always, with her familiar grin. Annette wasn't sure if it was her grandmother's words or the weight of the world that had caused her shoulders to sag, but there was no arguing with her.

Grandma Joyce looked every bit the part of someone ready to support her grandchild in any way possible. She had on her usual weekend attire—an oversized floral blouse that was a little too bright for early morning, faded jeans, and sturdy shoes that made a quiet thudding sound on the ground with every step. Her silver hair was pulled back into a neat bun, but the few strands that had escaped framed her face in a way that reminded Annette of the gentle, yet steady, nature of a lighthouse in a storm.

As usual, Ms. Castillo was waiting in the car, her same welcoming smile stretching across her face. *"Ah, I see the family's coming along today!"* she said, glancing from Annette to Grandma Joyce with a warm, almost relieved expression. There was an eagerness in her voice, a sense of wanting to make sure Annette had all the support she needed.

Ms. Castillo's hands were clasped tightly on the steering wheel, and she spoke with the slight bounce of someone trying to lift spirits. *"I'm so glad to see you both—really thought we might get this day started with just a little extra luck,"* she said as she handed them each a warm cheese Danish.

Grandma Joyce gave a slight chuckle, her eyes narrowing playfully. *"Thank you! They'll be needing more than luck, Ms. Castillo,"* she teased. *"You know Annette's got this in the bag."*

Ms. Castillo laughed, shaking her head, *"I'm sure she does, but it's good to have a warm cheese Danish around."*

Annette felt a small surge of warmth at the exchange, even as her nerves twisted in knots. She was grateful for the people in her life who showed up for her in ways that mattered, even when the world seemed impossible to navigate.

Annette sat in the car, staring at the entrance of the venue. She had made it to the last day.

"Breathe," Ms. Castillo said softly. *"You got this."*

Annette nodded, inhaling deeply before stepping out of the car. As she disappeared into the building, Ms. Castillo and Grandma Joyce sat in the car, parked near the entrance. The rules still barred spectators due to COVID-19 restrictions, so all they could do was wait.

After 2 hours, they pulled into a nearby Panera drive-thru, grabbing coffee, a breakfast sandwich and fruit cups before returning to the parking lot of the arena to wait some more.

"She's really something special, huh?" Ms. Castillo mused, taking a sip of her coffee.

Grandma Joyce chuckled, unwrapping her sandwich. *"Always been that way. Even as a little girl, always getting in the way, always asking questions."* She shook her head, smiling. *"Yes indeed, that child has always been in the way,"* she mused fondly. *"Always under my feet, sweeping when the floor don't need sweeping, digging in my garden pulling up the wrong things. But she's got a heart as big as this world. Always trying to help. I remember when she was five, trying to help me sweep the porch. Kept making a bigger mess, but Lord, she tried."*

Ms. Castillo laughed. *"Sounds about right. In my class, she was always first to volunteer for a challenge. She was always the one helping the other students. Explaining things in ways that even I hadn't thought of. Not just smart—she's got an imagination. She's innovative. Creative. A thinker. Finds solutions in ways other kids don't."*

Grandma Joyce nodded, her face turning thoughtful. *"She's different from the others. A blessing to this family. Ain't like the rest of 'em. Not saying the others ain't special, but Annette? That girl's got something different in her. Always wanted to help. Even in church, always offering to pass out hymn books. Didn't matter that the other kids didn't care. She just... does things her own way."*

Ms. Castillo sighed, watching the competition building. *"I've taught a lot of bright students, but Annette? She stands out. She doesn't just memorize things—she **understands** them. She's the kind of kid who could change her life with the right opportunity."*

Grandma Joyce wiped her hands on a napkin, looking out at the sky. *"I just hope she knows she don't have to carry the whole family on her back."*

A silence settled between them. They both believed in Annette, but deep down, there was an unspoken doubt. How could this girl from one of the most underprivileged communities in the state—no private tutors, no expensive prep courses—really pull this off? Was sheer determination enough?

They weren't sure. But as they sat there, waiting, they both silently hoped that maybe, just maybe, Annette was about to prove them wrong.

They hadn't heard a word from Annette since she went in, and the clock on the dashboard seemed to tick louder with every passing second. The minutes stretched on, longer than they had expected. Grandma Joyce fidgeted with her napkin, her eyes darting to the door every time someone walked by.

Then, suddenly, Ms. Castillo's cell phone buzzed on the seat between them. She grabbed it quickly, glancing at the screen before answering. *"Hello?"* Her voice was steady, but there was an edge to it, a hopeful anticipation.

"Ms. Castillo?" The voice on the other end was muffled but clear. *"We need you to come inside now. The competition's wrapping up, and we need you to mask up and come in. You're with Annette's family, right?"*

Ms. Castillo's heart skipped a beat. This was it. They were finally going in. Her eyes met Grandma Joyce's, who raised an eyebrow in silent question. Without a word, Ms. Castillo nodded.

"We're on our way," Ms. Castillo replied, hanging up the phone.

She looked over at Grandma Joyce. *"It's time. We've got to go."*

Grandma Joyce quickly opened the car door then stood, slowly, the weight of the moment pressing down on her. Her heart was beating a little faster than usual, a mix of nerves and excitement. It felt too real now, too close, and she wasn't sure if she was ready for whatever might come next.

Together, they moved toward the entrance of the competition hall, their footsteps quickening with every step. Inside, the hall was eerily quiet, they thought. The chairs were pushed aside, the large screens displaying the final standings—none of the other students were left, except for Annette, who stood near the front, looking small in the sea of empty seats. The stage lights were dimmed, but she stood there, like a solitary figure in the middle of a storm.

As they walked in, the person in charge, a tall man with glasses and a suit that looked a little too formal for the occasion, turned toward them with a wide grin. *"You have a winner!!"* he announced, his voice loud and enthusiastic, reverberating in the otherwise silent room.

For a moment, Annette couldn't process the words. Her chest tightened, and she felt like the room was spinning around her. Had she actually done it? Was this real? It felt like a dream. She glanced at Ms. Castillo, then at Grandma Joyce, who had her hands pressed against her face, eyes brimming with tears.

Grandma Joyce started crying, her shoulders shaking as she let out a choked sob. *"Oh, my God, baby... you did it!"* she whispered, her voice barely audible as she moved toward Annette, arms wide open.

Annette felt a rush of emotions flood her all at once—relief, disbelief, joy, fear, gratitude—all tangled together in one overwhelming wave. Her legs felt like they were made of jelly as she stumbled forward, barely able to keep herself upright. It was like the earth had shifted beneath her feet. She had really done it. She had won.

The person in charge gestured for Annette to come closer. *"Congratulations! You are officially the winner of the competition. Your $50,000 prize is set to be distributed by Tuesday at the latest. The funds will be transferred directly to the account your mother provided."*

The team had reached out to the phone number provided on Annette's application and reached Sherry. They informed her of the results of the competition and made sure the appropriate banking information was collected. In addition, they had explained all of the relevant information regarding the prize money, holding the phone so long, that Sherry was numb by the time the call ended.

Annette's mind raced, trying to absorb the magnitude of it all. $50,000. Enough to pull her family out of debt, enough to fix their immediate problems. Enough to give them a chance at something better. The money would be there by Tuesday—less than a week away.

As she turned to face Grandma Joyce, who was still wiping tears away, she felt a deep sense of accomplishment, mixed with a wave of guilt. *She didn't have to carry the whole family on her back*, she thought. *They were carrying her, too.*

Ms. Castillo placed a hand on her shoulder, her voice low. *"You've made history, Annette. Do you realize that?"*

Annette swallowed, her throat tight. *"It doesn't feel real,"* she whispered.

Grandma Joyce, who had composed herself for the moment, stepped forward, wrapping Annette in a tight hug. *"Baby girl, you just changed all our lives. You don't even know what you've done for us."* Her voice cracked, but it was full of pride, of love, of relief.

The person in charge smiled at them, giving them a moment to savor the victory. *"You'll be hearing from us soon about the official ceremony, but we wanted you to know as soon as possible. This is a huge accomplishment."*

Annette barely heard the rest of his words. She was still processing, still feeling the gravity of the moment. It had been so surreal—one moment, she was just a girl in a competition, and the next, she was holding the key to her family's future in her hands.

It was only when they stepped outside that the reality began to settle in. The cool evening air hit Annette's face, and she took a deep breath, as if she had been holding it in for months.

"We're going to make it, Grandma," she said softly.

Grandma Joyce smiled through her tears, her hands on Annette's shoulders, squeezing gently. *"Yes, baby. We're going to make it."*

And for the first time in what felt like forever, Annette believed it, too.

———————

CHAPTER TWELVE

NEW FOUNDATIONS

The air felt different that morning. It was a subtle change, a lifting of the heaviness that had hung over Annette's family for what felt like forever. The weight of the past few months—the chaos of her father's sudden death, the unraveling of everything they had once known—still pressed on them, but it was lighter now, as if they could finally breathe again.

Annette stood in the front yard, watching the sun filter through the trees, her mind racing with everything that had happened in such a short span of time. A few months ago, she had been just a regular middle school student, her biggest worry being homework and making it through the day without feeling invisible. But now? Now she was someone the world had come to know, her name splashed across headlines, her story of triumph against all odds holding the kind of weight that made people pause and take notice.

The local news had made her the subject of their morning segment, *"the young girl who had won an international math competition during a global pandemic, whose $50,000 prize had saved her family from ruin."* The interviews had been quick but intense, reporters eager to capture the miracle that had unfolded in their own backyard. Annette's story was the kind of thing that made people believe in the impossible. The kind of thing that made hearts swell with pride, even if they didn't know her.

She was grateful for it. Grateful for the attention, for the way people were looking at her with respect. But the truth was, none of that mattered as much as the weight of what she had done for her family.

Annette had paid the bills, the past-due rent. She had bought a car—nothing flashy, just something reliable that would get them from one place to another. She had finally been able to buy the headstone her father had deserved but never got. And, perhaps most importantly, she had been able to buy her siblings the things they had always wanted but could never afford.

But in the midst of all the chaos and relief, there was something Annette couldn't shake. It wasn't about the money, or the accolades, or the gifts. It was the fact that the family was still broken. The grief from her father's sudden passing still lingered in the corners of their home, a silence that hadn't quite been filled. And even though they were no longer on the brink of losing everything, Annette knew it wasn't enough to just survive. They had to rebuild.

Sherry, too, had been feeling the strain, the emotional toll of carrying everything on her own shoulders after Lawrence's death. But today, Annette noticed something different in her mom's eyes—something like determination, like she had finally decided that enough was enough.

"Annette, let's go," Sherry called, stepping outside. There was a subtle energy in her voice that Annette couldn't ignore. She followed her mother to the car, sensing that this wasn't just another day.

As they drove through the streets of their town, past the familiar corners and neighborhoods that once felt so permanent, Annette felt a flicker of hope she hadn't allowed herself to feel before. The memories of her father's dreams for the family were always there, lingering in the background, but now, they felt real again.

When they reached the lot, Annette's heart tightened. It had been so long since they had stood here, on the land that Lawrence had bought years ago, with the dream of building a house. He had talked about it endlessly—how one day, they would have a home, not just a place to stay, but a real home. A place that could withstand the storms of life. A place where the family would be together, no matter what happened.

The land was empty now, the foundation of that dream still unbuilt. It felt both like a weight and an opportunity.

"Mom," Annette whispered, standing beside her mother as they looked out over the lot. *"You think we can still make it happen?"*

Her mom's eyes softened, and Annette saw something shift in her. *"We will,"* she said, her voice steady. *"We're not giving up on this. Your father worked too hard for us to forget about it."*

As if on cue, Annette's siblings appeared behind them, exiting Matthew's car. Jordan stood quietly; his gaze fixed on the horizon. Chris was busy texting, but even they paused long enough to glance at the empty lot.

"We've got a long way to go," Annette said, her voice thick with emotion. *"But I think we can do it."*

Sherry turned to face them all, her eyes hardening with resolve. *"We're going to make this happen. And you know what? We're going to make it even better than Dad could have imagined.*"

And just like that, the dream that had seemed so distant —so out of reach—was back within their grasp.

The next day, Annette's mom took her by the hand and led her to the bank. Together, they began the process of mortgaging the land. It wasn't easy—nothing ever was. But the steps they took that day were a foundation for something much greater than just bricks and mortar. They were building a future, not just for themselves, but for the memory of Lawrence, too.

Annette stood beside her mother, feeling the weight of it all settle into her bones. They weren't just surviving anymore. They were moving forward. And this time, they weren't doing it alone.

The bank was cold and sterile, the air conditioning humming like it was trying too hard to mask the tension in the room. Annette sat across from her mom, the hard plastic chair pressing into her back as they waited. The anticipation of what was about to happen hung in the air like a thick fog, and Annette couldn't help but feel the weight of the moment.

Sherry, usually so calm and collected, had her hands folded tightly in her lap. Annette could feel her fingers twitching, the nervous energy coming from her like static. This was the beginning of something monumental—the start of a process that would eventually lead to them building and owning a house, but it felt so much bigger than that. It felt like a chance at a new life.

"We're going to do this, Mom," Annette whispered, leaning slightly forward, her voice steady despite the tightness in her chest.

Her mother turned her head and smiled softly, a small curve of her lips that didn't quite reach her eyes. *"I know, baby. But it's hard to believe, isn't it? We've been talking about this for so long... sometimes it felt like it was all just a dream."*

Annette reached over and placed her hand on Sherry's. *"But it's not a dream anymore. It's real. And we've got a lot of good things going for us."*

Her mother gave a small, acknowledging nod, her gaze shifting to the bank lady who had just approached their table. The young woman, a recent college graduate by the look of her, smiled warmly.

"Good morning! How can I help you today?" she asked, her voice cheerful and professional, though it did little to soften the tension.

"We're here to start the process of mortgaging this land," Annette's mom said, her tone clear but firm. She spoke like a woman who had already decided the outcome, as if this was a mere formality. But Annette knew better. She knew how hard this was for her mom.

The lady nodded, clicking away at her touch tablet. *"Got it. We'll need to go over a few details and make sure the land is properly appraised."* She glanced at them both before continuing. *"It won't be a fast process, but once it's approved, you'll be able to start moving forward with building your house."*

Sherry leaned back in her chair, exhaling slowly. The weight of her exhale felt like a sigh of relief, but there was still an edge to her voice when she spoke again. *"It's been so long since we even thought about this. I didn't know if we'd get here, you know?"*

Annette smiled softly, squeezing her mom's hand again. *"But we're here now. And we're doing this together."*

The woman smiled sympathetically. *"It's always hard at first, but once you're in the system, it'll be smooth sailing. Now, let's go through the paperwork."*

As the lady began outlining the details, Annette tuned out the technical jargon, her thoughts drifting back to the days after her father's death. How her mother had been so lost, so unsure of what to do. She had done her best to hold everything together, but the truth was, they had all been spinning—drifting through a world that no longer made sense. It had taken time for everyone to find their footing again, to rebuild the strength to stand tall.

And now, they were finally doing it. They were finally stepping back into the world of possibility.

———————

That evening, after the bank meeting, they went to dinner at a small diner. It wasn't much, but it had become their spot—the place they went when they had good news to share or when they needed to remind themselves that there was always a little bit of joy to be found, even on the hardest days. Annette's siblings had been restless all day, excitement coursing through them in waves. It was hard to sit still, knowing that everything they had worked for was finally starting to pay off.

"We really did it, didn't we?" Jordan said, eyes wide as he poked at the mashed potatoes in front of him.

"We're doing it," Annette corrected softly, offering him a smile. *"This is just the beginning."*

Sherry nodded, her expression now one of quiet pride. *"We've always been able to make things work. And this time? We're doing it better."*

Chris, who had been quiet all evening, finally spoke up, their voice low but full of feeling. *"I'm just glad to know we're finally going to have our own forever home."*

Annette's heart softened at her sister's words. She knew what it felt like—the sense of constant instability that had come with so many moves, so many changes. This house, this dream, was the thing that would finally give them all a place to hold on to.

"Hey, it's not just about the house, you know," Annette said, her voice firm but gentle. *"It's about the family. We've got each other. That's the most important part."*

The table went quiet for a moment, everyone processing the weight of what Annette had said. The truth was, they had all been holding on to each other, even when everything else seemed to be falling apart. They had become stronger through their struggles.

"Yeah, you're right," Matthew said softly, a small smile tugging at the corner of his lips. *"We're family. And we're gonna make it work."*

Annette felt a sense of pride swell within her. This wasn't just about saving her family from financial ruin —it was about something deeper. It was about learning to trust again, to believe in the future. She hadn't just solved their immediate problems; she had set them on a path toward healing.

In the days that followed, the family began to see the fruits of their labor. The paperwork with the bank had been completed, the mortgage application approved, and they received word that construction could begin once the permits were finalized. It was a slow process, but it was happening. Their dream, once a whisper of possibility, was becoming tangible.

There were moments of doubt, of course. They all had them. But every time one of them faltered, the others were there to pull them up. Sherry began making plans for the house, providing the blueprints that Lawrence had designed, sketching out landscaping ideas and talking about what colors they wanted, what furniture they would need. It was the kind of conversation Annette had never thought she'd hear, the kind of conversation that felt both surreal and wonderful.

They went to the lot often, watching as the foundation was laid, and soon enough, they could see the skeleton of their home starting to take shape. With every brick, every beam, every nail, it became clearer that they weren't just building a house. They were building a future.

And for Annette, that was the greatest victory of all.